ROUND TRIP
The Emigrant's Journey

Horácio Bento de Gouveia

Translation by Violet Long

2016

Violet Long was born in England and got her first degree in Modern Languages from the University of Bradford, with an emphasis on translation and interpreting. She went to Colombia as a volunteer to teach English and got her Master's in Linguistics at the Universidad del Valle. After teaching linguistics in Colombia, she obtained a Ph.D. in Sociolinguistics from the University of St. Andrews, Scotland. She has taught in Palestine, Bahrain, Cyprus, England, Italy, France, Portugal, the U.S.A. and Spain, where she returned to translation. She now lives in Maia, Portugal, and works as a freelance translator from Spanish, French and Portuguese to English.

NOTE – Before she translated this novel, Dr. Long visited Madeira, spending a few days at the Solar do Ladrilho – Casa-Museu Dr. Horácio Bento de Gouveia in Ponta Delgada.

Editor: Maria de Fátima de Ornellas de Gouveia Soares

Title: ROUND TRIP – The Emigrant's Journey

Original Title: TORNA VIAGEM – o Romance do Emigrante
1st Edition – 1979; 2nd Edition – 1995
3rd Edition – 2016 (English version)

Artwork cover design by João Ornellas

Book design and publication by Ana Isabel de Ornellas

ISBN-13: 978-1530496082
ISBN-10: 153049608X

Printed by CreateSpace, an Amazon.com Company
Mar2016

Available from Amazon.com, CreateSpace.com, and other retail outlets

1. Horácio Bento de Gouveia in his study.

Horácio Bento de Gouveia was a well known writer not only in Madeira, where he was born (1901-1983), but also around the world.

He was a writer and a teacher with a degree from the University of Lisbon.

He began writing and publishing at an early age as a journalist with newspapers in his native Madeira (1918).

Later he became a full-time teacher in various high-schools, both in mainland Portugal and on the island of Madeira but he never lost his qualities as a novelist and maintained a permanent collaboration as a journalist with the "Diário da Madeira" and "Diário de Notícias" da Madeira.

He wrote some poetry but mainly prose. He was born and baptized in the old Church of Senhor Bom Jesus in the small hamlet of Ponta Delgada, São Vicente, and is buried in the local graveyard. His gravestone is inscribed with the words he wished to perpetuate:

«ESTOU MORTO, E ESTOU VIVO...»[1]

---

[1] *"I'm Dead, and I'm Alive"*

INTRODUCTION

Professor Francis M. Rogers (1914-1989) mentioned Horácio Bento de Gouveia in his book *Atlantic Islanders of The Azores and Madeiras* (1979). As the grandson of immigrants from the Azores, it was his heritage that made him study and lecture on Portuguese language and literature in the Department of Romance Languages and Literatures of Harvard University.

In chapter 21 – High Culture (*pp. 391-397*), Horácio Bento de Gouveia is referred to as one of the most valuable writers of the 20th century:

"A Madeiran example is the novelist Horácio Bento de Gouveia (born 1902) who in 1976 had the satisfaction of knowing that one of his novels, *"Águas Mansas"*, of 1963, had appeared in a German translation as *"Stille Wasser von Madeira"*..."

The following is an extract from Professor Rogers' work, including his own translation of extracts from the works of Horácio Bento de Gouveia:

"... in 1966, the Junta General of Funchal itself published Bento de Gouveia's collection of short prose pieces entitled *"Canhenhos da Ilha"* (Memories of the Island), with its poignant description of the island,

'...lacking the resources needed by the humane agglomerate dispersed throughout its flatland, ridges, valleys, and mountain slopes. And the peasant, descending from the sierra with his bundle of beech sticks for the beans and occasionally stopping to rest at the turns in the paths, casts his glance at the sea horizon and, in spite of himself, begins to feel the winged impulse to disimprision himself in a search for lands where life would be less harsh.'

"The author then goes on to tell of the move by many Madeirans to Hawaii and quotes an 1880 letter from Honolulu back home. He concludes the piece: *'Yesterday it was Sandwich, today Venezuela.'*

"During the long years of the Salazar/Caetano dictatorship, Madeiran creative literature tended, in my view, to flourish a little more fully than Azorean. The physical features of Madeiran living, such as the rugged, mountainous, precipitous terrain, the lack of adequate pastureland, the need for an extensive irrigation system, and the cultivation of grape vines on terraces up the side of hills provided authors with forces to blame for the difficulty of life, as in the passage just quoted. *"Still Waters"* itself opens with an indication of the labor required to keep the water flowing in the *levadas* in the burning-hot month of St. John.

"On the island of Madeira, then, man's great adversary was Nature, the land itself, the hand of God. In the Azores, by way of contrast, Nature or God behaved differently. Relative to Madeira, the Azorean islands are natural paradises for man, gently rolling, fertile, well-watered lands for fauna and flora. Man's adversary in the Azores, probably beginning as early as the fifteenth century, was man. Azoreans, more obviously than Madeirans but no more so in fact, have been held down by the exploitation of a ruling class. In a two-class society such as existed in Portugal, writers under the monarchy as well as in the early and middle-twentieth century did not criticize members of their ruling class with impunity. Azorean writers chose instead to cultivate other themes, isolation and the concomitant monotony, the terrible storms, the perils of whaling, although throughout both Azorean and Madeiran literature, and Cape Verdean literature as well, the general parallelism of themes is striking.

"On Madeira, where the hand of an upper class continues heavy, Bento de Gouveia has dared go beyond Nature to man. In 1975, the third edition of one of his novels was issued by a well know publisher in Coimbra. It was entitled *"Canga"* (Yoke), and it was about the socioeconomic system known as the *colonia*. This word is accented on the *i* and is not the much-used word *colónia* "colony", written with an acute accent mark over the vowel which receives the main stress. A *colónia* is what Angola and Mozambique were. The *colonia* was as system of *colonos* or tenant farmers on Madeira. The *colono* worked the land owned by the *senhorio* or lord of the manor:

> 'Under the **colonia** system, if the lord is inhuman, the **colono** is one of the most miserable beings on earth. If the former does not permit the **caseiro** [literally the dweller in a **casa** or house, another term for **colono**] to enlarge the house in which he lives, which frequently occurs, he is responsible for the spectacle of a promiscuous life of parents and children in a single living space. It is a question of the demoralization and desegregation of the family. If perchance the **caseiro** does not please the **senhorio** under any circumstance, the latter pays him his benefices

and expels him from the home. This kind of despotism leads to emigration and to misery.'

"In an introductory statement, of which the preceding is the last paragraph, Bento de Gouveia provided a description of the *colonia* contract between *senhorio* and *colono* as it existed in the seventeenth century. In neither the first edition of the novel (1949) nor the second edition (1960), however, did this indispensable explanatory statement appear. Moreover, the title conferred on the book in those days of national censorship was simply the patronizing *"Ilhéus"*.

"Bento de Gouveia's three important novels – the third centering on the backbreaking labor which embroidering entailed – were all published in Coimbra on the mainland. Their author is therefore more than a figure of Madeiran literature. And so it goes with many other fine writers, both Madeiran and Azorean. They belong to Portuguese literature, not a regional literature..."

The opinion of Emeritus Professor Francis M. Rogers is for us of the utmost importance as he was a profound connoisseur of Portuguese culture, had done field research in Portuguese-speaking countries around the world and remained very aware of the evolution of Portuguese social, economic and cultural activities over more than 30 years, even after retiring from Harvard.

Professor Rogers' last lecture at Harvard University as the first Nancy Clark Smith Professor of the Language and Literature of Portugal took place in 1981.

A few years later, Professor Gregory Rocha (1922-2001) in his Ph. D. dissertation for the University of Harvard quoted and referred to the books and work of Horácio Bento de Gouveia. Professor Rocha was the founder of the Portuguese Studies Program at the University of Massachusetts – Dartmouth.

Horácio Bento de Gouveia's unusual writing style is known as *"Escrita Bentiana"*[2], and features in one of the courses at the University of Madeira.

As it is now difficult, if not impossible, to find new editions of Horácio Bento de Gouveia's original books, some universities in the United States have recently digitalized them, to make them more easily accessible for students of Literature and other interested scholars.

One of the difficulties that a writer faces when transcribing "language peculiarities", as in the case of Horácio Bento de Gouveia, is the Madeiran dialect: whether to transcribe exactly the sounds the people make, to give

---

[2] ...from *Bento* de Gouveia, "Bento's writing"

the "color" of the place, in other words, the special way that people talk in the different regions, on the islands and in the hamlets, even on a small island like Madeira, or, for example, on São Miguel Island in the Azores. The writer therefore has to make a decision. And Horácio Bento de Gouveia's decision was not to write anything other than the common language. He felt that the plot and theme of the novel and the way the action is presented by the author are sufficiently interesting for people to read it just as it is.

The old mansion, shown below, where Horácio Bento de Gouveia was born, stands in a small hamlet in the north of the island (Ponta Delgada, S. Vicente, Ilha da Madeira). After his death on 23rd May 1983, and following his own *"long lasting will"*, work was done to turn it into a museum, the: *Casa-Museu Dr. Horácio Bento de Gouveia*.

2. Casa-Museu Dr. Horácio Bento de Gouveia

We are also continuing to give the general public an opportunity to get to know my father's writings, which were scattered throughout the local newspapers, by gathering and publishing them each ten years period[3].

The idea of enlarging the readership to include young people made me think of translating some of my father's novels. I had in mind the sons and grandsons of immigrants from Madeira and the Azores living in English speaking countries, in the U.S.A., Canada, South Africa, Australia and the U.K.

This new generation does not know what the lives of their ancestors were really like. They had to leave their homeland in search of better living conditions for them and their families, to go to other, more welcoming countries.

Maria de Fátima de Ornellas de Gouveia Soares
December 2015

---

[3] See last page

IN PURSUIT OF THE VENEZUELAN DREAM

Horácio Bento de Gouveia (1901-1983), a native of Ponta Delgada, a village of the northern side of the Portuguese island of Madeira, is the most prominent Madeiran writer of the 20th century. During his lifetime he published several major works such as *"Ilhéus"* (1949), *"Lágrimas Correndo Mundo"* (1959), *"Águas Mansas"* (1963), *"Canhenhos da Ilha"* (1966), *"Alma Negra e Outras Almas"* (1972), *"Torna-Viagem – O Romance do Emigrante"* (1979), *"Margareta"* (1980) and *"Luísa Marta"*, published posthumously in 1986.

Gouveia's literary world revolves around the Madeiran reality of his time, both in his native Ponta Delgada or in Funchal, the island's capital, and in his novels one can find the portrayal of several topics such as the long exploitation of the peasants by the land owners, the dark side of embroidery industry and emigration. A peculiar feature of his characters is the way in which they speak, for the author presents their dialogues in an almost phonetic transcription, thus contributing to the preservation of several expressions of the Madeiran unique dialect.

Emigration is a common word in Madeira's history throughout the centuries. Due to the limited size and resources of the island, the continuous increase of its population, the oppressive land exploitation system, poverty, the lack of job opportunities, several economic crisis, among other causes, the islanders always sought a better life abroad. Since mid 19th century Madeirans are known to have emigrated to several destinations such as Trinidad, Demerara, Sandwich Islands (nowadays known as Hawaii), Brazil, United States, Curaçao, South Africa, Venezuela, among other destinations. Around the mid 1900's Venezuela was the favorite emigration destination for thousands of Madeirans, who saw it as their *Promised Land*, a country where they could make all their dreams come true and therefore a better living for themselves and a brighter future for their children.

Having witnessed the emigration flow of many of his fellow countrymen to this South American country, Horácio Bento de Gouveia wrote a novel about this topic entitled *"Torna-Viagem – O Romance do Emigrante"*, published through Coimbra Editora, Lda., in 1979, as afore mentioned. This novel had a second edition, by Editorial Correio da Madeira, in Funchal, in 1995. And now, through the tireless efforts of Gouveia's daughter, Maria de Fátima de Ornelas Gouveia Soares, the third edition of this book, entitled *"Round Trip – The Emigrant's Journey"*, comes to light.

It is to underline that this is the first novel by her father that has ever been translated into English and published in the United States, thus giving the opportunity to a brand new audience to get acquainted with this literary masterpiece. An as far as we know, this is the first book written by a Madeiran writer that has ever been translated and published in English. In other words, the present publication is an important milestone to Madeiran Literature.

This novel is divided in two parts, entitled, respectively, '*Unknown Lives*' and '*The Emigrant*'. In the first one a set of characters, among which Artur and Maria Clara and Francisco and Inês, can be seen living their hard lives in the remote area of Achada do Castanheiro, in the village of Boaventura, in the northern side of Madeira Island. The countryside life, with its joys and sadness's, is vividly depicted through Gouveia's chosen words. Most characters lead a hard life, having to work very hard to get the daily bread. Artur is a cobbler who hardly makes enough money to survive, and Francisco, a former peasant, buys a country store in order to improve his life, but soon discovers that it doesn't make enough money to pay for the expenses of running it. So they

3. An old photo of Achada do Castanheiro, Boaventura, the home of all the main characters of the novel.

both decide to emigrate, Artur to Brazil and Francisco and his wife to Venezuela.

In the second part of the novel one can see the different lives these characters led abroad. Being a womanizer, Artur soon forgets about his wife and children, who were left behind at Boaventura, living in extreme poverty, and wastes all the money he earned in Brazil with different women and after some years decides to move to Venezuela. Francisco, on the other hand, manages to climb the social ladder in this foreign country, through hard labor, becoming a successful business man.

When Madeirans emigrate they always have in mind returning home one day, with enough money to buy a piece of land and building a nice home in their native village, where they would spend the rest of their days in tranquility. And that desire is expressed by both characters. Artur returns to his native village of Achada do Castanheiro, almost empty handed as when he had left it decades earlier, and resumes his former occupation. Francisco and his wife, on the other hand, return to Madeira, but establishes himself in the capital of the island, buying a nice house at the fancy Avenida do Infante, thus showing their new social status, and opening a supermarket in Funchal with a business partner.

When they left the island, decades earlier, they both shared the hopes and dreams of succeeding abroad in order to escape poverty and provide a better future for themselves and their children but they both chose different paths in life. Artur despised his wife and children for years and years whereas Francisco remained faithful to his beloved Inês and led a happy existence. Like many Madeiran emigrants who pursued the Venezuelan dream, in the end it all had to do with the choices made in life. Success never came easy to any emigrant and was only achieved through hard work and determination of achieving this goal.

4. The church of Sta. Quitéria, in Boaventura, Madeira

Through the reading of *"Round Trip – The Emigrant's Journey"*, by the celebrated writer Horácio Bento de Gouveia, one gets a vivid picture of Madeira in mid 20th century. Although a fictional work, this novel is enriched by many details drawn from real life that the reader becomes one with the writer and becomes a witness of an era of golden dreams for many islanders.

Duarte Mendonça
Madeira Is., Dec. 2015

13

ACKNOWLEDGMENTS

To Dr. Violet Long, who as a native speaker kindly translated this novel into English. To Mr. Edward Jardim, an American journalist, who helped in revising "Round Trip".

To Mrs. Ana Isabel Ornellas and Mr. João Ornellas (my children and the writer's grand-children) who graphically organized this edition and created the design for the cover of the book.

And, last but not the least, to the writer and friend Mr. Duarte Mendonça who willingly produced the magnificent preface.

Maria de Fátima de Ornellas de Gouveia Soares
December 2015

In memory of my father,
Francisco Bento de Gouveia

In memory of my late lamented friend,
Dr. Francisco de Sousa Falcão

Now the LORD had said unto Abram, Get thee out of thy country, and from thy kindred, and from thy father's house, unto a land that I will shew thee.

Genesis 12:1

Literature is the domain of the unstable, a mirage of eternity that hovers over the passing years and centuries. On the human scale, it is an absolute: it remains and it passes by.

Jacinto do Prado Coelho

PART ONE

UNKNOWN LIVES

CHAPTER I

"I'm going to emigrate! I'm going to emigrate!" said Artur to himself, as he sat on his black linden wood three-legged stool re-soling some leather work-boots.

He did not feel that he was fulfilling his ambitions. At an early age he had started work as a shoemaker's apprentice, earning tuppence and feeling like a fine fellow because of it. But he always felt an emptiness, something missing from his life. He rarely ran around with the other boys from the village. His life was like the morning light in May when the sun's rays coloured the white-washed walls of his room red, bursting with creation, the origin of the world. Something inside him was pushing him on, but he didn't know where or why. When he was just an adolescent, eighteen years old, he set up his own shoemaker's shop on the main street of the village. It was manual labour in a poverty-stricken little shop with no escape from reality, but he was independent. However, his cash box was never full, except on feast days, when there was a pilgrimage.

The years passed. He did not prosper because the old-established shoemakers got all the customers.

Around the place where he lived were high rocks. Some had fallen on top of others and were covered in heather. The beech, mahogany, laurel and ironwood trees that grew there were like the columns of a primitive shrine, with its nave roofed over by the branches of the ironwood trees and walled in by the trunks of the trees. Artur lay on a bed of leafy branches on top of some moss, dozing, after tying up a bundle of firewood. Later, he carried it on his back to the little backyard behind the kitchen and threw it on the ground. With the help of his mother, Hermínia, he piled up the branches against the fireplace wall and then they fed the fire that was burning between the stones that held up the rusty iron cooking pot.

When the winter night fell early over the village, not the bleating of a goat or the barking of a dog could be heard. The wind blew in through the cracks in the kitchen wall. Artur was sitting on a three-legged chestnut wood stool beside his younger brothers, who were nodding off to sleep. He did not take his eyes off his mother and said to her:

"My job brings in very little. If I make a pair of cordovan leather boots, by the time I've paid for the materials, what's left over doesn't even pay for a pair of trousers!"

"Son, we were born poor but you can still be rich. The laws of the world are God's and not Man's."

"But good luck goes to those it wants to! It's not coming to me."

"None of that. Look at the Adriano's. They could only go up the mountain but they worked so hard they're rich folk today."

"I'm still young. One day I have to get on that boat. Out there you can earn a lot."

"That's true. If one day you leave us…well, it's going to be very hard for your father and me, but try your luck."

"When will that be? I like living here too. I like the neighbours. Here in Achada I like everyone and everyone likes me. And you've seen how my godmother's daughter, Maria Clara, has grown into a pretty girl, when only two years ago last Easter she was always coming to ask me to play hide and seek[4] with her. I'm amazed when I see her!"

"She's a good girl! And her parents have something!"

"They may be rich but that's nothing to me. Maria Clara could be my fortune."

"Artur, go and enjoy yourself at the festivals in other villages with other girls. It's still too soon for you to get tied down."

"Oh mother! I'm not saying that I want to marry Maria Clara! We're just talking."

---

[4] Translator's note: This particular game of hide and seek, called "belamente" (literally, beautifully) in Portuguese, is played by two or more people at Easter time. The aim is to win a pre-arranged number of almonds. Those playing hide two or three times a day and whenever they find each other they say "belamente". The one who says it the most times is the winner and must give the other player or players the number of almonds agreed on.

The wood burned under the cooking pot. Dinner was nearly ready. A cricket was chirping, lamenting the passing of summer. On the pine shelving on the wall, held up by two long nails, a long line of ants was moving along the edge of one shelf, some going, some coming, without colliding, day and night, on their journey to survival. They were an example of the fight to live, a mute, silent march, completely unaware of Man's battle for the same thing, of his pre-meditated effort. In both these creatures the goal was the same but the one was compelled by instinct and the other by both instinct and reason. There were Artur and his mother, living in their world of dissatisfactions, unaware of the world of the tiny creatures for whom space is also the path to life and death.

"The wind has got up, mother. There go our chestnuts!"

He could hear the nearby line of chestnut trees rustling in the gale.

"The chestnuts're still very small and they won't fall. But the wind is stronger than people."

"What a racket the rain is making on the tin roof!"

"Your father shouldn't be long. He'll be like a drowned rat!"

"Where did he go this afternoon?"

"To the Curado's house to get osiers. I told him not to be long. The darkness of the sky and the mountains was a sign of rain. And the path from Igreja to here… there isn't a worse one."

Now the deafening voice of the wind could be heard, swearing and blaspheming, denouncing the fury of the gods at the superstitions of the people. The soul of the rustic family has ancestral roots.

"Son, God sends the storms that ruin the crops because of our sins."

"Who'd think that so much rain and wind could come from the sky! The path is like a river. I'm soaking wet!"

Artur's father took off his dripping coat and threw the sack that he had tied on his head into a corner.

"Didn't I tell you not to be long? Come and warm yourself by the fire. I'll go and find you a shirt and some trousers."

"If it hadn't been for Mr. Curado giving me a glass of wine and talking so much, I'd have come home dry! It's a fair way in this weather from Sarrão to Achada! And the worst thing is, if you get sick, where's the doctor?"

"You have to go to Santana. More than a three hour's walk!"

"It's as black as pitch! If it wasn't for the lantern that Mr. Curado lent me, I couldn't have come home tonight."

The conversation was interrupted by the howling of Valente, who was clawing at the kitchen door.

"The creature's all wet! Poor Valente!"

And Hermínia took the pot off the stones. She ladled the cabbage and potatoes onto the plates with a wooden spoon. With the howling of the wind and the sound of the rain, supper was accompanied by the same topic of conversation: the rain, the wind, the trees, the crops and the cattle.

At forty, Hermínia was tall and thin, with a long dark face, brown eyes and dark hair. Her husband, Leonardo, was of medium height, with a heavy body and prominent cheekbones. He was older than his wife. Artur was like his mother in the looseness of his body.

The vicar, a friend of his, was teaching him to read, write and count.

The winters passed by with their long nights and short days. The nights felt even longer because of the high mountains that were anxious to touch the sky with their massive, jutting peaks, covered in vegetation that was born, grew, multiplied and died of old age. These were the mountains that closed in Achada do Castanheiro: mountains soaked by heavy, year-round snow, with sheets of water from the torrential rain, a place where the springs that fed the streams arose. The environment of this lonely place called out to its inhabitants and shaped the way that they were; their souls lived in their bodies but were also formed by the mountains, the vegetation, the silence and the wilderness. Even though sometimes Maria Clara was restless and outgoing and could not help wanting to talk, more often she had an expression on her face of uncalled-for sadness, as if the soul of the nature around her had penetrated through her skin and into the most sensitive fibres of her romantic depths, which were overwhelmed by the limited horizons and the deep undergrowth nearby. Her rustic surroundings shaped her reactions and her feelings.

"My heart is sad!" she said to her mother countless times.

Her mother used to reply, "So, what's wrong, girl?"

"Nothing's wrong!"

"You're just being silly," was the affectionate end to the short dialogue with her daughter.

***

The early evening of the day before the feast of Sta. Quitéria was engraved on Maria Clara's memory like an inscription carved in stone.

In the centre of the churchyard was a fair packed with regional articles: tablecloths, embroidered handkerchiefs, rugs, skeins of wool, things made out of wickerwork, from simple chairs to ones with backs fashioned by baroque hands. All around, on the edges, the steps were hidden by the throng of people who were leaning back on them and on each other. In groups, the girls from the villages round about, wearing short skirts made of flimsy, pale coloured fabrics and no stockings, were gossiping and laughing. The boys hung around the edge of the churchyard.

Artur arrived at the fair. When Maria Clara met him by chance, she offered him a series of raffle tickets for a pretty tablecloth made of local linen.

The curious and the interested were elbowing each other, all talking at the same time. Artur raised his arms in a gesture that asked for information.

"Is that the tablecloth?"

"Yes."

"Just look where I'm pointing."

"It is that one!"

Artur bought all the tickets. And the wheel with the numbers spun round. One voice stood out from the others:

"35! Number 35 wins!"

Maria Clara, smiling with her lips and her eyes, carried the folded tablecloth over to Artur. Without anyone hearing, he whispered to her, "Wait, it's for you! Don't ever forget who gave it to you." And the expressions in their eyes as they met said more than words, as if they had spoken.

And this was how love was born in a simple country churchyard strung with flags, in the same way that marigolds and four-leaved clovers spring up along the capricious, meandering path from the church to Achada that people had traced along the riverbank. That was why the evening before the feast was engraved on Maria Clara's memory like an inscription carved in stone.

When night came, like a silk fabric trimmed with violets falling over what lives and does not live, the strings of multicoloured lamps that criss-crossed the churchyard and formed a latticework were lit. The crowd of pilgrims grew in size. There was a constant bubbling up of little groups, the yelling of small boys who were holding the sticks of the spent rockets that they had picked up on the paths or in the fields, after the salvos that had echoed from dawn to dusk. Round and round the fair went a wall of people that did not stop. The churchyard was full of people. But, in the midst of the throng, Artur stood like a statue under a chestnut tree. He was following Maria Clara's smallest movements. His eyes did the talking.

Two o'clock in the morning. Like a line of ants, the crowd of villagers from Achada climbed the path along the banks of the Moinho river. A lantern with the dim light of a candle led the walkers and guided them but from time to time Artur lifted up his arm above his head so that the light would prevent them from stumbling on the loose stones on the uneven ground in their shoes and leather work-boots. The water ran between the willow trees. The syncopated song of a shearwater cut through the air near the mountain. The onomatopoeic voice of the bird broke the silence, mimicking the syllables of its local name: "*pa-ta-ga-rro... pa-ta-ga--rro...*"

"Can you hear it? It sounds like it's on the mountain!"

"No. It's in the ravine. It's going to drink some water," said Inês from Lombo.

"It's evil! That means someone will die..." stammered Guilhermina.

"Who told you that, girl?" asked Artur.

"Don't you know? My grandfather used to say that one night he was out watering the beans when he heard a shearwater singing on the ridge of the Levadeiros' house. The sons came out into the street and threw stones at it. But it didn't do any good. Next day Levadeiro died."

"Now I'm sorry I came," said Maria Clara.

"Then you're going to hear another story as true as the one you just heard," exclaimed Rafael.

"My uncle told me that some time ago a certain Canheiro lived in Arco de São Jorge with his family, his wife, two daughters and three sons. One starless night, a shearwater that sounded crazy was going up and down screeching 'pa-ta-ga-rro'! Then it couldn't be heard any longer. But when they least expected it, they heard 'pa-ta-ga-rro' coming from the rooftop of their house. One of the sons grabbed a beanpole and hit the damn' bird. The next night, the sons were again woken by the sound of 'pa-ta-ga-rro'. They got out of bed and went to get the shotgun. They fired one shot but the bird flew away. Two days later, Canheiro died."

While the words drifted away into the past and stopped being sensational, the time passed and the sleepy-eyed pilgrims arrived back at the sleeping square, where the loneliness of silent things reigned. The new moon was rising over a mountain peak.

Artur hurried to accompany Maria Clara to her door. She had to go around the grape arbour and a barn with walls that were almost falling down, one of which was bulging out misshapenly. Anyone who passed by there said the Lord's Prayer so as not to die buried beneath the stones.

The lantern lit the way. But ever since she was a child, Maria Clara was used to the irregularity of the ground that had never been smoothed by the hand of Man and she arrived at the door of her house without the aid of the lantern.

"You see! I didn't need your light!" she exclaimed, smiling.

"But I need the light of your eyes."

"Ah! Whoever said that only just noticed that I have eyes!"

"So you didn't know that the eyes say more than the lips when you start to like someone?"

And the conversation continued while the night was still behind the mountains.

It was not easy to go to sleep. She was filled with excitement. The memory of Artur filled her thoughts. And she thought about how peaceful she had felt before the fair, before he gave her the tablecloth. Now she felt a change in herself. She could not sleep for thinking of him. How strange it was. She could not explain the attraction between her and the boy. When she was small and was playing among the pine trees, her brother had stuck a pruning knife into the bark of a really big tree and the sap had begun to seep out. Another time, when Artur had gone to Cabo da Ribeira with them, she had put her finger in the sap and two of her fingers stuck together. Artur had done the same thing.

"Why does it stick?" she asked him.

"Look, I don't know," he replied.

Now the scene came back to her, ten years later. The sap was like glue. And she still didn't know why it stuck to your fingers and hand. Artur was like the sap; he was stuck to her. But what was the sap? Was it liking him? Maybe, she finally decided. And she fell asleep to the strangled crowing of the cock.

***

When Artur got home to his vine-covered house, he took the key out of his right hand trouser pocket, put it in the lock, turned it and opened the door. He went into his room and lay down on the bed. He could not sleep because his thoughts were too confused. He could not stop thinking of Maria Clara's face. Her scornful words rang in his ears: "You only just noticed that I have eyes!" In reality, he had known her since she was a little girl. When they used to go to Cabo da Ribeira to gather myrtle for St. John's Day, to decorate the house, he didn't notice the girl's eyes. And once they went to the pine woods with her brothers.

He had never noticed the colour of Maria Clara's eyes; never before had he felt the sensation that they now produced in him. Maria Clara was right when she was surprised that he had never mentioned her eyes. He excused himself; he was still young, he was a long way from the age for love. There was no way he could sleep. The night seemed endless. He asked himself when daylight would come. The desire to see her again occupied every moment of his thoughts. Now his only reason for living was wanting to see her again. Why? To be with her. He didn't want to know anyone else. Achada do Castanheiro existed because Maria Clara had made it exist. And with some complete thoughts and other incomplete ones, the language of love expressed itself in his naturally crude mind in one short phrase: he liked Maria Clara. It was this liking that contained the exalted sentiment of passion, the passion that Artur was rapturously living, the onset of a burgeoning love that was indelibly marking his consciousness like the brand on a cow's skin. This was not a sinful love that would overwhelm the enchanted glow awakened by a specific being and arouse the sense of touch, but the desire to gaze piously at the image, not the flesh and blood person. He was at the spiritual stage that lives for the abstraction rather than the possession of the object itself.

Finally, his eyes closed. However, soon after, the sun, bright and unconcerned, came in through the panes of the window and touched the little mirror on the wall that hung from a rusty nail on a piece of string. The intense light woke him. But it was Sunday; he didn't have to hurry to get out of bed. Again, Maria Clara occupied his thoughts, which were aflame with an affection he had never experienced before. And so the courtship began.

But who can trust his own heart? If life is change, constancy and steadfastness are stable now, but later they are not. Permanence definitely does not exist. Feelings change as the affection that captured them is transferred from one object to another.

The feast of Sta. Quitéria was followed by that of Penedo, some months later, in the little chapel that was made picturesque by its surroundings: peaks covered with cultivated fields and trees encircling little hills.

On the eve of the feast day, Maria Clara got ready to go to the chapel with her mother and sister. Artur could not go with her. The sun was already going down when they left. Along the way, they pulled aside the wild brambles on the edges of the hillside. When they came out in the churchyard, there were crowds of people. They went up to a stall. Inside were a boy and three girls. Maria Clara casually looked into his eyes, which were staring at her. She felt a shiver run through her. It was the strangest thing in her life. With Artur, it was different, calm. But the other boy's eyes were a fire, a flame that lit her up inside. She couldn't take her eyes off him. She felt a weakness in her body, an indefinable relaxation. The attraction disturbed the serenity of her soul.

While the band was playing on the bandstand, the boy kept Maria Clara in sight. Now here, now there, now closer, now further away, to avoid arousing the suspicions of her mother and sister. He was of medium height, dark, with a thin face and came from São Jorge. Some relatives of his father lived in Penedo. Maria Clara had not seen that face at the feast of Sta. Quitéria, either in the churchyard or when leaving the service. Wherever she went under the arches of flowers and among the stalls, whenever Maria Clara stole a glance, she met his eyes, which were following her movements. She couldn't understand what was happening.

Once, when her mother and sister stopped to talk to the Curado ladies, she went over to a sweet stall and the saleswoman sold her a dozen fennel sweets, which she bought because she liked them best. Just as she was going back to her mother, she heard right in her ear: "I want to talk to you". She jumped. Her feet seemed to be glued to the ground for seconds, but she did not stop walking and he continued to follow her surreptitiously, sometimes almost touching her, at other times moving away when a space opened up and there was nobody there, striking a certain pose so that she would notice him. Maria Clara was living a reality outside of reality. One reality, there under the little coloured lights, was feeling the boy's bravado; his penetrating look was a flame that burned her and forced her eyes to follow him as if enchanted. The other reality was the life that she led in Achada do Castanheiro as the girl who was courting Artur.

As soon as the boy from São Jorge went away to the bazaar, Maria Clara daydreamed about it, without finding a reasonable explanation for her giving herself up to someone that she didn't know at all. She was only aware of the feeling that sprang from her heart and her virginal body and overwhelmed her. But it was difficult to define this feeling because one moment it made her forget the solid affection that she had thought she felt for Artur, more solid than the mountains round Achada, and the next she wanted to be close to that other man, without knowing why. She had never felt like that with Artur. She remembered Sta. Quitéria's day, the raffle, the engagement that would end in marriage. All this unexpectedly caused a change in her, not in her intention to start a family in the future, but in her whole being, a desire to sin, to feel that boy who fascinated her caress her body. She couldn't explain the reason for this instinctive attraction to someone she had just seen for the first time or the indifference that she felt when she thought about Artur, who stroked her face every day.

It was past midnight when Maria Clara and her family joined the small group from Achada do Castanheiro and, with a lantern in front and the chords of a badly tuned guitar breaking the thick silence that covered the dark mountains and the cavernous riverbank, they went down the narrow path.

As they walked down the path, Álvaro, the boy from São Jorge, taking advantage of the crowd of people that pressed up against the group that included Maria Clara, took hold of her arm. She turned her head and a glance from her eyes betrayed her instinctive passion.

***

Weeks went by. The boy, whose name was Álvaro, found out by careful enquiry that Maria Clara lived in Achada do Castanheiro. He was the son of well-to-do parents and spent his time wandering around from sunrise to sunset having easy little adventures with peasant girls who had nothing to lose. He kept away from those who had not been ruined as he did not want to marry anyone. But he was obsessed by the memory of Maria Clara. He thought for days on end about how he could go to Achada without anyone finding out that he was there. Finally, he thought up a reason: to ask the person there who did the most delicate work to embroider a table cloth that his mother had bought in the city.

One morning in September, he left the village, went down the narrow, winding Entrosa trail, climbed São Cristóvão and, when he reached Igreja, followed the path that opened up like a narrow crack between the rocks to the first cottages, the vanguard of the village of Achada. He stopped and looked around. There was a house a few metres away and another farther off. So, he carried on walking. He stopped in front of a cottage that had a small yard bordered with flowers planted in rough beds built on the steps. He looked around again. On a slope near the house, a small woman was hacking at a patch of brambles with a sickle. He went up and asked her if she knew anyone who could embroider.

"Yes, sir."

"Where?"

"Right here. Clarinha has lovely hands. And Josefinha is really good at making buttonholes."

"So what would you advise me to do?"

"Maybe ask Clara. I don't know if she would take any work from a stranger... She's going to get married."

"Is she at home?"

"If you like, I can call her."

"Well, thank you."

The little woman left her sickle next to the patch of brambles and disappeared behind the house, which had a window open on one side.

Walking slowly up and down, Álvaro thought agitatedly how wonderful it would be if Clara was the girl who had made him go crazy on the eve of the festival in Fajã do Penedo. And if she really was the one who came out, she would be amazed to see her lover and worried about what the family would think. But the idea of the tablecloth he wanted to have embroidered was a good reason for his being there. As he was thinking this, the door opened. A head appeared. And since Álvaro was looking toward the door, their eyes met.

"Excuse me, but I've been sent about some work for my mother." Her face reddened and, confused, she did not reply immediately. Suddenly she reacted,

"What work?"

"A table cloth to embroider."

"Let me see it."

"I didn't bring it with me." And he whispered so no one could hear, "I came looking for you. I like you."

She was silent. She felt suffocated by the heated voice that was speaking to her and his ardent look. And without waiting for him to go on, she said:

"I'm engaged! Don't think about me anymore."

Álvaro, excited by the presence of the woman who had upset his peace of mind, impetuously grabbed her hands and kissed them greedily. Then he took her in his arms and their bodies touched. Becoming aware of the situation, Maria Clara pulled away and closed the door. After a few minutes of indecision, she came to the window in a feverish state and called out:

"Sir?"

He left the doorway and stood like a statue by the corner of the house, sorry for his impulse, which had really been instinctive.

But when he heard her calling to him, he went over to where the voice was coming from.

"Bring the tablecloth." And she stepped back from the window.

While this was happening, Inês, who was coming back from washing clothes in the river, saw the stranger, a good-looking youth wearing dark tan shoes and a black felt hat. She was startled. What was he doing there? Whose house had he come to? The puzzle was easily solved. As she neared the yard of her house, she met Rosa, who, without being asked, said, "There was a lad here looking for an embroidress and I told him about Clarinha."

"Where is he from?"

"He doesn't sound as though he's from Boaventura."

"He must be from over by Arco!" guessed Inês.

"We live on those mountain tops and there's always someone who needs us."

"Even from the city, it's only peddlers who come here. The well-to-do don't normally come here on foot," replied Inês.

Álvaro, eaten up by passion, wanted to stay there forever, seeing his beloved all the time, like a part of himself, wanting to be the tree and her the clinging ivy, to make her beautiful, as without her his life would be incomplete, a life with no colour, no sense and no harmony. He assumed that she would be the world, his world: the bed of wild flowers that would have as its centre the flower of the flesh, sex, the human flower, the only reason that his sense of touch could imagine. He was a visionary, but seeking a real body with all its reactions, rather than the Petrarchian beauty of the ideal woman.

When he came back to reality, he saw that he was surrounded by some small boys who were staring at him with all the natural curiosity of an uneducated childhood. He thought then that he was out of place there in Achada do Castanheiro. Having decided this, he left. The group of gapers didn't move, they continued to stare after Álvaro in amazement, shocked after spending their lives shut away in rustic solitude. Walking along, he looked down at the ground between the flower beds and felt obliged to trudge on, following the winding path that had been so seductive when he started out to find the woman he loved. He told himself that he was going into exile, away from the love that he had to conquer to make himself the owner of the beauty of an unequalled body.

The sun was setting in a blue sky when Álvaro arrived back at his village, passing between the hydrangeas that grew on either side of the path, which was straight and flat in places and wound in lazy curves in others. When he got home, he went into the kitchen and saw Emilia, the housekeeper's daughter, a dark haired girl to whom he had promised marriage in exchange for a kiss from her pouty lips. She knew his wiles and went out with her eyes fixed on the ground as soon as she saw him.

But now the reason for his existence was Maria Clara. And the night after he went to Achada da Castanheiro, Maria Clara was the central character in an erotic dream.

It was the evening before a festival. Maybe he was reliving the memories of the one in Penedo. She was at home alone. It was a moonlit night. He left the village when it was growing dark and by the time he got to Achada, the moon was just peeping over the pine trees on the slopes of the mountains. Maria Clara was waiting for him by the half-open door. He put his arm around her waist and their mouths met in an endless kiss. Then they fell onto the soft mattress. He could feel how warm and soft her legs were. Her heart was beating and her virgin breasts were pressed under his.

He woke to the sound of her mother's voice saying, "Maria Clara, open the door."

The dream revealed a repressed desire because he did not finish the act of possession that slept in the depths of his memory. Once he was awake, he was excited by a false reality, pictures that faded like smoke or slid away like foam. But the images sharpened his desire to touch her as he had in his dream.

Next morning, as the sun was rising, Álvaro went down into the yard and found the cock with a red crest covering a grey feathered hen under the vines. He compared the animal's instinct with his own and decided that there was nothing wrong with the inevitable attraction that drew him to Maria Clara. He began to search for a way to go to Achada do Castanheiro without being seen, even if the pretext was the tablecloth to be embroidered.

"Here are the pears."

This short, unexpected phrase caught his attention. The housekeeper's dark-haired daughter put a basket on the windowsill in the kitchen and moved aside. Now his attention was caught by the flesh-coloured pears, which looked almost artificial. He took one and bit into it. He didn't notice the taste because his thoughts were not on his senses but on the persistent, blinding vision of a woman, a female waiting for her man.

The sound of the words, 'here are the pears', rang in his ears but he did not notice the girl's presence. So, dwelling on an image that make him almost unbearably anxious, he put his hand into his jacket pocket, pulled out his diary, opened it, leafed through it and saw that the week was almost at an end: Friday. He thought to himself, "Tomorrow, Saturday, if it doesn't rain, I'm going back to Achada."

CHAPTER II

In the yard in front of the cottage, daisies were growing by the wire netting of the corrugated iron roofed chicken coop. On the opposite side of the yard, a pig was grunting, penned in by pine poles. When the instinct moved him, he pushed his snout into the stone trough filled with potato peelings and chaff. The oldest boy in the family was running around barefoot, propelling a small iron hoop with a thin stick ending in a wire fork. Here and there, beyond the flat clay field, fences of luxuriant maize that oozed sap separated the isolated houses. The sky above Achada do Castanheiro was full of the thick, grey clouds that darkened the September evenings, shortening the days and making the night come sooner and the chickens roost earlier on the poles that criss-crossed the chicken coop. There was a vague scent in the air, carried in on the breeze from the tree and bramble covered land that already smelled like autumn. The mornings were still muggy from the long summer. The dampness could be felt on the skin, the dampness from the low snowfields.

The wet purple eyes of the daisies closed earlier too as the afternoons grew shorter.

"The bunches of grapes are black. When do we harvest them?" Inês asked her husband.

"You're the one who knows. Did you talk to Adriano about the wine press?"

"No."

"Then talk to him as soon as you can, because if it rains, we'll only get a barrelful instead of two casks."

Inês had married Francisco Freitas seven Christmases ago. It was on a beautiful, sunny March day when the mountains could be seen clearly and a little breeze was gently moving the leaves on the bushes in Cabo da Ribeira that Francisco asked her to marry him.

She was collecting wood for kindling and he was gathering grass for his calf. Inês had not been expecting this declaration and was left speechless, but after a few moments she told him that she was not old enough, to which he replied,

"I'll talk to your father."

And so two simple souls were united. They came from the rough virgin scrubland that was beautified by the river valleys, the encircling mountains and the birds that sang hymns of praise to procreation.

Although they lived in a thatched house with the plaster falling off the walls and strong winds whistling through into the bedroom, Francisco never cursed his luck. His ambitions were limited: for his family to be healthy, for his little fields to continue to be fertile and produce enough for them all year round so there was never a shortage of food for the pot, and to raise his children to work. He did not mince words. He was not talkative. Like all country folk, his speech contained the words *this thing* and *that thing* and frequently used one particular noun, *thing,* so common in that social group. But he did not voice his thoughts until he had thought hard about the point of them, especially if it involved responsibility or might be a worthless opinion. Despite his easy-going nature, which adapted to circumstances as they came up, not everything suited him. When he felt that he had been hurt by someone, out of spite, his rage made itself felt. This had happened because of a savage incident involving the pretty little calf a few months old that Francisco affectionately called "My Blackie". When he got to the door of the barn, it was enough for him to say the name of his Blackie through the hole in the wall to hear the sound of a tail beating on the side of the manger and the gentle voice of the animal responding to its master's call. The calf knew the sound of his voice, like a puppy. Francisco was so taken with him that before opening the door to give the grass to the animal, he would stand there like a statue, leaning against the rough stonework, pondering, uncomprehendingly, the workings of non-physical life and its irrationality.

The barn was on some sloping ground in Lombadinha, far from the houses. Many times, on the nights when the winds blew hard and she was alone with Francisco, talking to him before going to sleep, Inês used to say,

"There goes the barn and that calf."

"Be quiet."

"How many times have I told you to bring that little calf nearer to the house?"

"Yes. And where's the barn?"

"You can take down the one in Lombadinha, bring the stones down here and build another one."

"It's alright saying that."

"Well, we're going to have a problem because of that barn being so far away."

And she was right. Her clairvoyance was never wrong.

In the farthest slums of Cabo da Ribeira, where all you can see is the mountain and the sky, lived the Ratazana family. The boy in the middle, who was about 12 years old, had a terrible character.

He would take the shears and if he felt like it he would rush at the hedges and cut down whatever he found: guavas, lemon trees and grapevines. But one day when he had hidden among the grapevines to cut himself some grapes, the owner suddenly appeared. This scene took place on the banks of the river. The boy's lynx-like eyes didn't spot Marques, a merchant from Serrão, who shouted at him furiously with the cords in his neck standing out:

"You wretch! You rascal!"

This stopped him. A woman who was weeding nearby stood up and looked aghast.

"You wretch! If I catch you, you'll get it!"

And Marques went after the young hooligan, who dropped the shears and ran away in terror, leaping over the boulders, to hide in the tangle of heath, beech and bay trees.

The merchant, who was exhausted from the effort of running, sat down on a tree trunk with his head in his hands to take stock. More than a hundred vines had been destroyed because their tips had been chopped off, while others had been cut in half. What was he going to do? The boy had inherited the destructive instincts of his great-grandfather. He needed to be sent to a reform school. But it took almost a day to get to the local council offices, if you went on foot, and the mayor lived in Rosario and almost never came to town. And complaints generally remained verbal because Marques couldn't write. He had been to school but, however much he wanted to learn, his father would never let him go alone in winter to Punta Delgada from where he lived in Falca. It took almost a day to get to the school, climbing up and down the mountains along paths that he had to hack at with a sickle to get rid of the thickets of brambles that grew, matured and wasted away up there. The north was ignored by the government. He'd heard it said that the island began to be populated in 1425. Five hundred years might have passed, but the north still didn't have any decent roads between the villages or from any one of them to the city. And Boaventura, where scattered families huddled in the folds between the jagged mountains, was more backward than the rest. This is what Marques was thinking. Knowing how to read and write was for those who had the good fortune to live in Igreja or not far from there. Although the distance to the school in the next village might only be a few kilometres, it was a dangerous journey, not because of bandits, but because the traveller had to contend with a narrow, steep path cut into the high, jagged rocks that rose vertically from the sea. It was so narrow that there was hardly room for people to walk in single file. And in the winter after the torrential rain they had to cross the streams that flowed down the slopes of the mountains and held up travellers for days on end.

So, Marques decided not to go and complain to the authorities.

Francisco thought about the conversation that he'd had with his wife that night when the devil was out, transformed into a gale. And he decided that she was quite right. In this life, who could boast of being sure of a day that he hadn't yet lived through? The future does not belong to Man and never has. Someone could steal his calf or kill it. Anything could happen. The greatest worry is always that something bad will happen when you're not expecting it, and that leaves a deep impression on people's memories.

So, the days and weeks galloped by for those who lived intensely, enjoying their physical and their inner lives. The days succeeded each other on the machine of the world, always the same, sunrise then sunset, because the earth is a top spinning in space just as Man does on earth.

In Achada do Castanheiro, Francisco was living in keeping with the reality of time. Francisco and the other country folk in his village, and in all the places where men feel close to the land, went from their homes to their fields. They went to the ends of their villages to find wood for the fire and grass for the cows and they took shortcuts to get to the barns with the livestock and to the paths that link the villages together. Being aware of time is remembering in the peace of the night just what one did in the morning and in the evening; being aware of yesterday, the week that just went by, a month ago, a year ago. Time lives in the memory as a concept that is shared but cannot be seen. Space, on the other hand, is made up of dimensions that can be seen and touched. It is a visible reality that lets us see both the parts and the whole. It is an outward experience that has length, breadth and height. Time is not like that.

Every day Francisco followed the winding path to the barn, dawdling along when it was only drizzling and hurrying when the drops threatened to become heavier.

"Blackie!" The gentle lowing of the little calf touched Francisco's heart. He unbolted the door and filled the manger with bundles of weeds that he got in Cabo da Ribeira. If his chores occupied him for the whole day, half an hour before the church bell rang for the "Avé Maria", he would go to Lombadinha and get back home just as night was putting out the light of the sun.

He lived a happy if monotonous life. If he had known how to write well and had enjoyed poetry, he would have been another follower of *"Aurea mediocritas"*, the golden mean: happiness is living in the country.

The story of the destruction of Marques's vines by the boy from Cabo da Ribeira spread quickly by word of mouth. Inês's husband was sitting in the doorway of his house when he heard about the wicked deed. He shook his head and began to imagine. What if he took the shears again to something else! What if he went into the barns and killed the cows! Anything could happen.

Francisco stood up, lifted his head and looked at the top of the chestnut tree where a blackbird was singing, perched on one of the highest angled boughs, which was scarred from being stoned when there were ripe chestnuts. Meanwhile, Inês arrived with a bowl of laundry that she'd gone to wash in the river. Her face was red from the effort of going backwards and forwards because the sun was already high in the sky. And she still had to make lunch.

"I talked to the men about demolishing the walls of the barn. We set a day."

"So you'll move the calf this week?"

"No. Only in a fortnight. Luís and Carlos have other work to do and they can't come now."

"You should have talked to them before. I do things faster than you. When I think of something that has to be done, I don't rest until it is done. I was always like that. You know that. Never leave till tomorrow what can be done today."

"What's necessary is not to forget things. Let the time come."

"Listen, you're wrong thinking that way. Last year, when the grapes were ready to be picked and you said that there was time, the rains came and we lost more than three barrels."

"You're more headstrong than I am," said Francisco.

In spite of being born in Achada do Castanheiro, the daughter of parents who only thought of living by the strength of their arms, fighting to dig the earth, ploughing furrows, spreading fertilizer, sowing seeds with the idea of getting a good harvest and having a pig and a cow in the barn to increase their income, Inês hoped for an easier life. Before she married, she took pains with her clothes. On Sundays and during festivals, she liked to be seen looking clean and different in a blouse and skirt that fitted her well and had no wrinkles. When she thought about getting married, she didn't have it in mind to get married just for marrying's sake. She wanted her husband not to be content to live like the people there, but to dream of being well-to-do, even if he didn't get rich, because riches are not for everybody.

So, she got married. During the first few years she talked to Francisco about their future there in Achada. Often in the kitchen, when the cabbage, potatoes and beans were cooking on the hearthstones, her imagination raced. Her face lit up with joy. If he opened a grocer's shop, their income and their situation would be different. But with their lifestyle and their few resources, a shop wouldn't be enough. She remembered Igreja, which was more of a village and had more population and a church to attract believers from all around. They came from the closest to the farthest ends of the parish: people from Pastel, Pomar, people from up in the mountains, people from Ribeira do Moinho, from Roçada, from Levada, Lombo do Urzal and other hamlets. As well as that, the centre of the parish was in Igreja; the post office was in Mr. Catanho's shop. These were excellent conditions for Francisco to do business and she was convinced that the experience of her going into the shop on a Saturday to go over the weekly accounts together would be productive. Four eyes see better than two. She became excited at the thought of the project. Her imagination was inflamed and excitement made her heart pound as she saw the reality that she hoped for reflected in the clear glass of her great desire. But suddenly the enchantment ended. It diluted like a drop of ink in water. She looked at the reflection of the same idea from a pessimistic point of view. The light of the morning sun turned into the dark of night. Her face took on a melancholy expression and her thoughts turned to the negative side. How many shops were there in Igreja? Silvestre's, Sousa's, Porfírios' and Hilário's, not counting the Curado's ladies'. Too many grocers, like too many taverns. And with another one, even if it did well, jealousy could bring it all down. And then there were those who wanted credit and with the credit there went the profit, like Abreu's shop. Poor thing, he had had to go back to farming. She had to plan another direction for Francisco's life.

Sunday would be the first day of the week for building the barn in the plot behind Inês's house. Saturday was coming to an end. It was a sleepy afternoon. And as the evening light was fading and nature was tiring, the bed of pansies and red roses that decorated Inês's modest house gave off a heady scent that revealed the soul of the flowers, and that of the gardener. How could one say that her spirit had not been permeated by the soul of the roses when it was her hands that had taken hold of the jug of water that afternoon and upended it on the roots of the flowers? Even when she was a little girl, Inês liked to plant flowers in the corners of her parents' yard.

And everybody in Achada do Castanheiro knew that the people who came from the city to the north in December to buy eggs called Francisco's house 'the house with the flowers'.

As Saturday evening was ending, the couple was leaning on the sill of the open window in the languor of the unusual peace of that dying day in May, so gentle and calm.

He exclaimed, in reply to her observation that the days were getting longer:

"How nice it is here! I don't feel like going to bed!"

That was how Francisco's crude brain expressed this spontaneous emotion. The sensations aroused by the poetry of the twilight were transformed into the word '*feel*' and expressed in the negative. But this state of consciousness was interrupted by the arrival of Angela, a neighbour who lived three houses away. She was coming back from Igreja, where she had gone to buy paraffin and two candles.

She blurted out, "A good afternoon to you! It's only a step there and back! But it took me nearly an hour because of the corns on my feet."

"What are people talking about down there?" asked Inês.

"I'll tell you something I heard in Hilário's shop.

"A woman from Seixal had bought some fish from some fishermen. They were three jack mackerels. When she got them home, she put them on the kitchen table on a dish. She didn't remember that the cat could get its claws into it. And she went outside to wash her husband's dirty clothes. When she went back onto the house, she was going to descale the fish. But where were the fish? She looked around and saw the cat chewing away on the biggest one. Without thinking twice, she locked the door from the inside, grabbed a stick and began to hit the cat, but the animal arched its back, jumped for her throat, dug its sharp claws in and she fell down on the floor. When her husband came home, he asked his daughter, who was playing outside, where her mother was. She said that she was in the kitchen teaching a lesson to the cat that had stolen the fish. He banged on the door but the woman didn't reply. He banged again. Nothing. So then he knocked down the door and there on the kitchen floor was the cat with its claws still in the dead woman's throat."

"Heavens! Can it be true? It's hard to believe," said Inês.

"Cats are very treacherous," replied Francisco.

"Even at home people aren't safe," said the neighbour, ending the conversation.

***

On Monday, as the sun was sliding up the side of the mountain, Francisco set off for Cabo da Ribeira with a rope and a sack. When he got to the little spring, he sensed something moving in the bushes. He went closer. He pushed aside the branches of bay at the entrance to a cave and looked in. It was a goat that had disappeared two months ago from Poio de Cima. He tied it up, picked some grass, bundled it up, put the bundle on his back, untied the rope that held the goat to the trunk of an old knotty vine and led it downhill to his house. The goat's eyes were soft, with almost human kindness. From time to time it stared at its new owner and stood still in adoration. Francisco tied the rope to the pigsty and when the goat saw the pig it began to butt him.

"Why is the goat butting the pig?" asked Inês's boy.

"Because a pig is a different kind of animal," said his father.

And the boy wandered off, grabbed his iron hoop and began to run along with it.

***

The stagnation of country life. Just the simple, daily routine. Everyone had just a few habits. And the least reactions caused a great concentration of accumulated energy. This was a world that knew nothing about the bubbling, artificial, jarring life of the city and its bastard language. At that time, the villages had not yet been contaminated by customs brought in by cars and buses and archaic expressions could still be heard in their purest form: 'to go to t'*ent o't*'river bank'; 'I *mizzed* thee', '*in t'meantime* he downed the pear tree'; 'I'm a-going *presently*'; '*thee found* the crook'[5].

In the afternoon, Francisco took the bundle of grass to his calf. He climbed up the steep and winding path in the silence that nature has given to the trees, the empty furrows in the fields, the earth's dry hair-do of weeds burned by the light of the sun and everything that does not seem alive but that emanates from plant life, which the human senses think is always silent. Overwhelmed by the uncommunicative afternoon, he walked along without thinking, in the sacred, August silence of the majestic mountains whose soul is silence itself.

Walking without thinking, he came to the top of the hill. He put the bundle of grass down on the ground and opened the door. He looked for the calf but then he wiped his eyes with the back of his hand to see better, as if he had been struck by a bright light. And then he saw it. The end of the calf's tail had been cut off with a sickle. He asked himself who was the scoundrel who had done this. And, as if on a cinema screen, the face of the rascally boy from Cabo da Ribeira came into his mind. But where was the evidence of this savage act! There was no proof. He searched all the corners of the barn in the hope of finding the sickle or the calf's tail. But it was no use. No sickle, no shears, no saw and no calf's tail. Inês was right. Why hadn't he built the barn near the house in time! The scoundrel would not dare to try anything there because he would be found out. The saying applied very well now: 'bolting the stable door after the horse has bolted'.

Weighed down by his bad luck with the little calf, he stroked the animal's flanks with both hands and his heart filled with anguish. Then he hurried back down the path so that night would not catch him far from home. He was filled with a desire for vengeance. All he wanted to do was to box the boy's ears. It couldn't have been anyone else. There had never been a family in Achada do Castanheiro that had such an evildoer.

So, he strode mechanically toward home, looking inside himself rather than observing where he was going, but not tripping over the stones because there weren't any. He opened his eyes, although they were already open, and saw that he was in the yard, where Inês was

---

[5] Translator's note. Here, northern English dialect is used in an attempt to give the flavour of the Portuguese accent of rural Madeira.

waiting for him anxiously. They had run out of paraffin and, since it was night, only Francisco could go to buy it at Silvestre's shop in Igreja.

"You're late home and I need paraffin."

"I'll go down to Silvestre's."

While Inês was putting wood between the hearthstones, her husband told her what he had seen, with disgust and hopelessness.

"I knew it in my heart!" Annoyed at what had happened, she didn't say another word. But she didn't go away so as not to make Francisco even more unhappy.

A cricket was chirping when he passed by the tumbling river, a bottle in his hand. As the cricket chirped, he was struck by a thought, a question with no reply, the same question that he'd already asked when he was in the vicar's class at school. Why do crickets hide in holes in walls? Why isn't man's life like that of a little insect that doesn't need bottles of paraffin to live? He didn't have a life like that! Why wasn't he born a cricket rather than a man?

He put these thoughts aside and lengthened his stride. Inês was waiting for the paraffin.

CHAPTER III

Maria Clara's and Artur's routines changed. Before they had started courting, he would go to the cobbler's shop at half past eight. Now at 8 o'clock she was waiting for him, sitting in the yard on a rough pine bench embroidering. And they talked until nine. Artur opened up the shop and Maria Clara would spend the morning doing household chores or very often going over to Inês's yard to embroider, as they were relatives, or to help her when she had a lot of work to do. Everyone in the village knew about their closeness and their courtship. No one talked about them in the neighbourhood except to praise the girl's qualities as one of the hardest workers around and one who had every virtue. About him it was said that he was crazy for festivals, not just the local ones but those in other areas, where he went on pilgrimages, singing and dancing and flirting with the wilder, good looking girls, in unrestrained self-indulgence. There in Achada, it was said that he would settle down in time, that he was sowing his wild oats, and to justify this opinion they pointed to Inacinho, from Travessa, who, when he was twenty, had his head turned by women so badly that one day he went off to the city, rushing down the tiring Torrinhas path to go and live with a fallen woman. But it didn't last long. A month later he came home, got married and didn't do any more crazy things, and it was said that Inacinho had been bewitched.

After Artur started going out with Maria Clara, he changed his ways. He gave up the habit of going off to enjoy himself at festivals. Nobody from Achada saw him on the eve of festivals, wandering around and joining up with groups of new-found friends in Arco, or wearing out his shoe soles on the steep paths to São Jorge, Faial or Santana. Now, as if he had made a vow, he no longer left his own parish to seek out sights and excitement at the festivals for the patron saints of the surrounding area. He only went out in the company of his girlfriend. Now, his enthusiasm was limited to the sacred and profane rites for Sta. Quitéria and Bom Jesus. Maria Clara stopped him from being headstrong. His parents could not contain their happiness at seeing him hanging around the girl next door like a sunflower following the sun.

Artur spent the whole week softening shoe leather, hammering it down to make new shoes or to mend old ones. He put several layers on the heels and steel protectors on the toes. Handmade shoes made little profit and even less now that readymade shoes were selling better. Most customers preferred shoes from the city that had been imported from manufacturers on the Continent. Cream leather work boots, which were cheaper, brought in very little profit. And the people round about, from Igreja to the peaks of the mountains, only wore cowhide boots with tyre tread soles as they stood up better to daily wear and tear and trudging over the old paths, those that had been trodden into the earth by long dead inhabitants. It is true that the custom of working in the fields barefoot was coming to end but even so what a shoemaker earned was not enough to fill the corner of the cash box. Black calfskin shoes with rubber soles were for Sundays and holy days as they were more elegant and more expensive. They lasted for many years. And after the war in Europe, there were more materials for shoes. Artur therefore thought about changing his line of business. After thinking about the kind of life he would adapt to best, while talking to salesmen from villages in the north and south, someone advised him to buy cattle for slaughter. Not only would he get the meat from the cows, he would also get good money for the hides. But since cattle were not slaughtered every day, he decided not to give up his shoe mending business. This decision certainly was the result of concentrated thinking about the future. So, the shop served as his office. There, customers would tell him about the farmers who had cattle and about the quality of the animals. And there, seated on three-legged stools, the buying and the selling of the cattle took place.

One afternoon at the end of November, one of those melancholy afternoons with thick, heavy fog that fills the deep, open valleys that lie around Boaventura, the sky was weeping because the vegetation had appealed to it when it was dying of thirst in the extremely dry months of spring and summer.

Artur looked out at the weather, leaning against the doorpost of his shop. Seeing its scowling face, he assumed that the deal had fallen through. Pimenta had promised to come and take him to his barn to see his ox, a new animal that had been well cared for and would give good meat and a good hide. He put his hand in his waistcoat pocket and took out his watch. It was past five o'clock. A muddy carpet of water was running down the street, which had lost its cobblestones centuries before. Only the voice of nature could be heard: the rain and the wind shaking the branches of the plane tree outside the door with all the strength of its invisible arms. Discouraged, Artur sat down at his bench, put a black calfskin upper on the last, took up his hammer and began to hammer in small tacks around the upper.

"Good afternoon, Mr. Artur. I almost didn't come! In this weather..." Pimenta closed his umbrella, which had a broken spoke and was dripping with rain, and leaned it against the whitewashed wall, with the end resting on the holey, warped pine floor.

"How much are you asking for the ox?"

"One thousand eight hundred. And that's cheap."

"Can't you take off a little bit?"

"Come and see the animal." Artur lowered the wick on the lamp. At half past six it was already dark so he lit a lantern, put on a coat and opened his umbrella. They went out together. As they went up the steep, hole-strewn path, with their boots splashing in water, the light pierced the darkness of the wintry night. The rain was falling hard on the ground and bouncing up again.

"Is it very far?"

"We'll be there in about a quarter of an hour."

There was no human presence to prove that there were any buildings up there, not even the barking of a dog to announce the presence of a house either close by or in the distance. After climbing still higher, when they rounded a sodden bend, the light from the lantern revealed a barn door made of cracked planks. Pimenta lifted the wooden latch on the door. They went in. The ox was lying on the straw but, disturbed by the dark shapes, it got up. It was a well proportioned animal that had been well cared for, with black and white patches on its skin. Pimenta stroked the animal, smoothing the hair on its flanks with his hand.

"I was telling the truth. He's worth what he weighs."

"I'll take him for one thousand six hundred."

"No, sir. Whoever buys him will make more than two thousand escudos."

"Fine. He's sold. Come to the shop tomorrow for the money."

And they went back down the path while the rain mocked them with its laughter and made the leaves on the bushes shine. Artur cursed silently because his trousers were wet where they met his boots. They followed the river-like path down to Igreja in single file. Their thoughts were similar, as they both were turning over in their minds life's bitter reality: living for money.

CHAPTER IV

The horizon turned blood red as the sun's crimson disk went down. Álvaro estimated that if he left then and walked fast, he could be in Achada in less than two hours.

The Little Dipper passed by, hunting for rabbits. Night fell. The bull's-eye lantern lit up the crumbling Entrosa path but its steepness and tight bends stopped him from running as he wanted to. So, thinking and planning how to talk to Maria Clara, he arrived at the first houses, which were already familiar. He put out the lantern. He came up to her house and knocked on the door. It was very dark and not even souls in torment were out. Only he was certain that he existed.

"Oh, my goodness!" Maria Clara shut the door and told him to talk to her though the window.

"Don't come back here. You'll get me into trouble."

"But I like you. Don't you see that I've come from São Jorge just to see you? The tablecloth was just an excuse."

"I believe you, but I have a boyfriend and if he sees you, it'll be bad for you and for me."

Without resisting, she let him kiss her hands. Afterwards, Álvaro stood on the tips of his toes to give her a long, hot kiss on the mouth. Suddenly, shaking herself, she said:

"Have some sense! This is bad for me."

"But I like you… I want to marry you…"

"Marry me! But I'm engaged!"

"So you like him more than me?"

"Someone's coming. Go away." But he kissed her lips again in a long, hot kiss.

The dark form stopped. Maria Clara closed the window. The person moved to the door and knocked.

"Oh, it's you, Artur! So you came today?"

"I didn't have any boots to work on."

Standing close to the threshold, he stood with Maria Clara talking about the future. Because she was his fiancée, he avoided testing the domination of his instincts, of his 'libido'. They would be married in a few months. Maria Clara also pulled back; she shied away from having her innocence put to the test and losing her virginity. The desire for initiation and the end of the beginning would take place on the wedding day. Until then, he remained stoical. His fiancée was like an image in a sanctuary, a sacred object that did not arouse any sensuality. She, on the other hand, did not understand her lack of sensitivity to Artur's hands. Her cool temperament was electrified and inflamed when Álvaro just looked at her in a different way from the other boys. She felt that his eyes made her senses boil as if they had touched her, and this never happened with Artur.

***

Among a small number of inhabitants, nothing happens in their lives that does not become known. Things that are repeated and are not noticed one, two or three times, do become noticed when they come together unexpectedly. Who doubts the maxim: '*the pitcher will go to the well once too often*'?

One afternoon, Afonso from Cabo da Ribeira went into Artur's shop and, taking his Sunday boots out of a sack, said that they were his only ones and could he please mend them by the weekend. Then he sat down on a bench and started talking. He talked about poaching, hens being stolen and breeding pigs.

"The nights are for banditry," stammered Artur.

"And also for those who dare to tempt the girls," said Afonso loudly.

"That's their fault!"

"It's not always like that. There's one individual, no one knows what parish he comes from, who was seen near Clarinha's house one night last week."

"Maybe he was looking for somebody."

"Or for something else!"

"What time was it?"

"I was told it was about eleven."

Artur said nothing.

"So, I'm off."

"The boots will be ready on Friday."

Artur sat thinking about the shadow he had seen that night near Maria Clara's house. There was no doubt that a man had been wandering around near his fiancée's house. It did not occur to him that she was involved. It could be her sister, despite her being fifteen. He thought it was late but he decided that he had to play the policeman and keep watch till after one in the morning.

In Achada, the march of time was moving more slowly. Little problems did not make it go any faster. From time to time, Ratazana's son got up to his tricks. The last one was to break the aerial cable used to transport brush and firewood from the mountain. It was quiet at night. The people shut themselves up in their tiled or thatched houses.

It was the time for flowers. The evenings were longer than in February. One night, Artur decided to go on his rounds as usual after dinner as the daylight finally faded. However, after talking to Maria Clara, he remembered that he had to finish mending some shoes for the following morning. He took the bull's-eye lantern and set off for Igreja. He put the key in the lock and went into the shop. After the work was finished, he followed the old path to Achada. He heard the sighing of the leaves on the windblown trees. Outside Inês's house he caught sight of the figure of a man walking slowly along the wall of Afonso's barn. Artur went round behind the newly built wall and from there watched the man sneak around behind his fiancée's house. Without losing any time, he followed him. Below the house, a terraced field formed a step. Artur sidled along the wall, putting one foot in front of the other. And he stood there with his head on a level with the upper step where the house was. He could just see the figure of a woman at the window, but not clearly. Everything was in darkness.

He was soon able to hear odd phrases but she was speaking so quietly they made no sense. In contrast, the man's words were clear.

"But I like you too!"

And Artur saw the shadow hold out its arms and the woman at the window lean out. While they held that pose, they stopped talking. His senses were on fire. He asked himself if he should step out and be recognised so that he could identify the two of them. But, if he approached, she would go in and the man would run away. It would be better to wait for him to leave and then, when he went down the path and was in some dark place, warn him or hit him. So, with a heavy heart, he left his hiding place. Seated on a rock on the river bank, he waited anxiously, in exasperation, for his rival, the cause of his amorous misfortune, and for revenge.

CHAPTER V

Inês did not talk to her husband about the incident again as any reference to it hurt him because it reminded him of his idleness over rebuilding the barn. What she could not stop thinking about was changing their lives from a hand to mouth existence to better conditions that were less tiring and brought in some money for those expenses that always come up, such as illnesses.

One week in January, she left the house and went to buy some odds and ends at Hilário's shop. His wife was behind the counter, looking very upset.

Inês could read the sadness in the woman's face and after going around the point she managed to get to know what was wrong. She found out that the woman's husband was applying for a passport to join a group of emigrants that were needed in Venezuela. The woman opened up and told her that they had to leave in fifteen days time and it was so hard for her to leave the shop, it was like one of the family. She had worked there behind the counter from morning till night for ten years, serving people with matches, foodstuffs, candles and paraffin. If there was anyone interested in buying the shop with the merchandise, her husband would sell it. Inês found out the number of customers and the credit that could not be avoided and, in spite of having given up the idea of a grocer's shop months ago, talking to Hilário's wife made her think about it again. And when Parruca's son came into the shop for a bottle of paraffin, Inês thought and thought again about the opportunity to make a change in how they earned their daily bread. A well organized business was tempting. So, resolutely, aware that the best supplied shop in Igreja had a great future, she said to Hilário's wife as she was leaving:

"My husband might just buy the business. Keep it for me until tomorrow. I'll tell you yes or no by midday on Wednesday at the latest."

"Think about it well so you don't regret your decision."

"How much are you asking?"

"My husband tallied up what we have in here and he told me he wouldn't sell it for less than six thousand."

"It remains as I said: I'll back here at the latest by noon on Wednesday."

And so Inês went back to Achada do Castanheiro. When she got home, Francisco was sharpening an axe to go and chop up some beech branches that he had brought down from the mountains. With a gentle smile, Inês said to him very quietly:

"We're going to change our lives. Leave the axe and come inside so we can talk."

Inês sat down on the bench in the kitchen next to Francisco and told him about the conversation that she had had with Hilário's wife. There had to be other people interested, but they wouldn't make a deal until after noon on Wednesday. They weighed the pros and cons and agreed to do it. They did not have anything like six thousand escudos but when night fell Francisco went up the path to Serrão where his godfather Andrade lived. He had gone to him when he was a bachelor and had never been refused a loan. His godfather dealt in vines and cattle. He combined luck with his expertise in making deals in the nearby villages.

When Francisco knocked on the door, a dyspeptic looking man with a heavy beard and rheumy eyes appeared, wearing a stocking cap and puffing on a pipe.

"It's you, Francisco!"

"Yes, godfather, it's me."

"Come in."

"My boots are wet."

"Come into the kitchen. It's warmer."

And without more ado:

"I came to you, godfather, because I want to do a deal to buy the lease on a shop and I don't have all the money."

"Which shop?"

"Hilário's."

"Ah, you're doing the right thing. Your wife, who's smart, will help you and you'll earn money with the business. How much do you need?"

"Four thousand."

"That's alright. Wait here for me."

The fire was crackling in the hearth and the woodchips and green twigs were smoking. Francisco rubbed his eyes with the back of his hands as they were watering. It was dinner time and Andrade's daughter had put some kindling and twigs under the pot as the branches of firewood were too thick to fit between the hearthstones.

"Here are the four thousand escudos. You'll pay me back only when the shop makes money."

"Thank you, godfather."

Next day, Wednesday, Francisco and Inês got up early and went to Hilário's house. He was not surprised to see the couple as his wife had told him that the deal was almost done. They talked. As a receipt, Francisco took the key to the shop and to all the stock. He was delighted at his bit of good luck, from which he could become rich. Thinking of this, the new owner of the shop went to Igreja. He went up to the door, put the key in the lock, listened to it turn and opened and locked the door several times. Wasn't he the owner? Knowing that he owned the shop gave him the will to triumph, to overcome the difficulties that always face shopkeepers when they start out. Inês swept out all the corners of the room, cleaned the spiders' webs off the ceiling with a broom and swept the floor. She wiped the counter with a cloth that she wetted in the stream that ran behind the shop.

Every day, without an alarm clock, Francisco got up at seven, shaved, washed in the china basin, dressed and set off to go straight to the shop. He opened both the doors. The customers would already be waiting for the shopkeeper to come round the corner. Many months had passed since the leaves had sprouted and only a few months were left before the end of the year, and the shop was better stocked than any of its competitors. So, on the eve of the festival, Inês had to help her husband. The four thousand escudo debt was down to a thousand. At the end of each month, when the books were balanced, the credit had taken more than half of the profits, even when there were no big payments to be made. Inês talked in vain to those who owed her.

"We'll pay at Christmas," said Parruca's wife.

"We haven't got the money yet from the osiers," moaned Anselmo.

And the others came up with excuses that they had to accept. If they had nothing to sell, the customers would go to Cambado or Passada or Carvalhosa. They also gave credit. Inês felt discouraged, full of dismay.

One Sunday night, when the shop was closed, Inês thought about what was happening. Leaning on the shelves holding the packets of pasta, she considered how once she had rejected the business for good reasons. Now she could not explain why she had decided that it would be a change for the better for her husband to buy the shop. If she and her husband had done like Artur did, only selling for cash up front and not even giving credit for repairs, the profits would have been enough for them to do better than their neighbours in Achada do Castanheiro and be the richest people there. She did not want any other happiness than this: to stop having a hard life, have a house with two storeys and send the children to school. But there they were, facing the payments for the tins of paraffin and the boxes of candles, quite apart from the sugar, the cooking pots and little things, and the cost of transporting the sacks and boxes containing the orders from the port to Boaventura. It was true that the children wore clothes made of the best cloth whereas before they had the shop, the eldest boy had always worn torn or mended britches and now he was wearing long trousers and no braces.

A knock at the door distracted Inês from her thoughts. A police corporal asked abruptly:

"Is Ratazana's son here?"

"No sir! But if you doubt me, take a look." The policeman was not convinced and opened the door that led to the storage space. He bent down to see if he was hiding under the counter. In vain.

"I'm sorry, but we have to catch that ruffian. He broke into Mr. Artur's shop and stole some calfskin boots."

"Why don't you go to Cabo da Ribeira where he lives?" asked Francisco.

"Who's going to pay for the trip? He's not my father's son! If the cobbler paid me something, then we'd see. But he wouldn't buy anyone a drink. I'm not leaving Igreja. Good night."

"You see that, Francisco? What good are the authorities?"

"Don't you see that one of the police corporals is from the village? And I even think he might be a cousin of Ratazana's.

"You're right. The authorities in one place ought to be from another."

Then, changing the subject, Inês asked:

"Did you get the cases of ginger beer? And the lemonade?"

"I didn't remember that Christmas was almost upon us and with the rough seas the ship hasn't unloaded."

"Do you think that it's worth it to give credit, Francisco? With all that credit, you can't get rich if you're born poor, as my father used to say. But I have to tell you that I've lost all hope of having a two storey house. The shop doesn't make enough! We have to find another way to make a living."

And the couple, their faces shadowed with sadness, foreseeing the destruction of their dreams in an unrewarding fight to the death, put out the paraffin lamp and were engulfed in the night. They were like pilgrims following a fantastic, lifelong vision there in Achada do Castanheiro, in a world with limitations for people but not for the dreams that Inês dreamed. Condemned from birth to live in a larger or a smaller place, one of Man's tendencies is to leave the smaller one and become the master of a larger one because it fits his ambitions for greatness, whether this greatness is defined or not.

Inês and her husband silently walked up the slope as the path grew narrower, turned to the right, carried on and ended in a funnel shape like a bird's foot. Although they did not speak, it was only Inês's words that were silent; her thoughts were tumbling over each other. For the first time, the desire to emigrate took hold of her. Francisco would try it out and later on, it would be as God willed. She thought to herself, where everything is small, one can't be big, but where everything is big, a poor person can become rich. Looking at it carefully, in Achada do Castanheiro everything is small. In Boaventura everything is small too, and even in the city, and what is the city in comparison with what is out there in the world?

Suddenly her daydream ended. Sitting on the step outside the door, their son, Carlos, was whimpering and pouting.

"Why didn't you go to bed?" asked Inês.

"I was waiting for you!"

Inês promised herself that this was not going to happen again; they were not going to come home late. The younger daughter was asleep. What if Carlos should get the idea of going down the path to meet his parents and he fell and hurt himself! They had not been thinking.

CHAPTER VI

A breeze was blowing off the mountains and Artur could not decide if it was warm or cold. He put his hand to his face and felt the heat of his skin. It was hot so the wind could not be cold. He was sitting on top of a rock behind a large thicket of vines, crossing and uncrossing his legs mechanically. As he listened to them, the seconds ticking by on his watch seemed like hours. What if he went down the shortcut to Igreja? he thought anxiously. But then he changed his mind because it was dark and only those who knew the way well would dare to do it. And then another idea came into his head: whether he should light the bull's eye lantern and, if he did, whether he could go along that dark track between the vineyards and bean fields. Anything seemed possible. However, as his thoughts were wandering restlessly, he heard footsteps coming round the bend in the path. It was dark. He recognized the figure by its height, thin body and the hat with the brim tilted down over the eyes. When the newcomer was within a half dozen metres of him, Artur stood up. Standing like a statue, fearlessly blocking the way, because the path was so narrow that anyone walking up or down it completely blocked it, he waited. Álvaro's stride shortened.

"Where are you coming from?"

"Leave me alone."

"No! Tell me where you're coming from."

Confused and upset, he stammered as if he normally did so. His mind had gone blank while he was uttering the first confident words of that unexpected meeting.

"I don't know!"

"You don't know? Just a while ago you were talking outside a window!"

"That wasn't me!"

"Liar! It was you! There's no mistaking that hat, or your clown's body. So, tell me, if you don't want me to break your nose!"

Álvaro was terrified and the truth came out as if he had been struck by a whip.

"Yes, it was me."

"Who were you talking to? Maria Clara or her sister?"

"The sister!"

He had hardly said the word when Artur gave him such a punch that he fell on the ground. And he said, "Boast in your own village about what just happened to you and to your own friends, as an example for them."

And he turned his back and walked away, his nervousness gone, enjoying his revenge.

With a bloody nose and an aching body, feeling sadder than death, Álvaro got up and stumbled away on the final leg of his journey home, a journey that had never been like this before, however bad, not because of the images but because of the sensations. The Entrosa path, with its many bends, seemed to be steeper than ever. He felt weighted down. He had not counted on someone's waiting for him, either a relative of Maria Clara's or her fiancé. It was his fault, because he had been warned that she was engaged, but because he was arrogant and full of himself, he went on courting her with no serious intentions. What most depressed him, and would ruin his reputation as a conqueror, was that the news of the punch that had left him helpless on the ground would go around the village. Now, everybody in Boaventura would find out about the incident and when he went to a festival or into a shop, people would snap sarcastically at him, "So, someone has finally taught you a lesson!"

At the age of almost thirty, this was the first bitter note in the history of his adventures. His pride was wounded; he had thought that he was physically invulnerable and could not be taken to task. At times, with these thoughts, the idea of self-annihilation occurred to him. But the voice of reason told him that over time, everything is forgotten.

When he got home, he went up the stone steps, took his key out of his pocket, put it in the lock, turned it and opened the door. His mother heard his footsteps. A mother's heart has a sixth sense that is rarely wrong.

"What happened to you? I was worried!"

"I was in Santana with Gil and Albino and the time passed without us noticing it!"

"It's two o'clock! You have to change your ways, son! You're almost thirty, of an age to get married." He did not reply. He lit the oil lamp and went to bed.

But when his mother went to take him some coffee at nine o'clock, she looked at his coat and saw that the back was smeared with mud. Something had happened. And she did not rest until she found out. Álvaro, however, invented a story, saying that he had slipped when going down the path to the river. The ground was wet. And he stuck to that acceptable explanation.

Artur could not sleep. He saw the scene at the window before his eyes. Álvaro was standing on his tiptoes as that was the only way he could kiss her. But to kiss who? Maria Clara? Her sister? That was the question that was on his mind and would not let him sleep. He wanted to leap out of bed at that late hour and go and beat on Maria Clara's door but at the same time he resolutely swore to himself that he would not go there until he had found out what had really happened. The man had to be from that lot from Arco, even if he was not certain. And he was sorry that he had not left him with a nice black bruise on his face. But speculation and unsubstantiated ideas kept providing excuses for the man's actions. If he was standing talking at the window, it must be because the other person, who was leaning out, had agreed to it. If she had already been married, she would not have been there to cause upsets, with or without a reason.

Morning had broken when he got out of bed and looked out of the window at the view. Trees clung to the basalt rock of the mountains and stopped them from eroding. He decided not to go and see Maria Clara.

The days of the week went by. Some days after the event, people were whispering about the incident on the path and the reason why it had happened. It had seemed that there were no witnesses, but even in the smallest hamlets not everyone goes to bed with the chickens. Someone saw something. So, by Friday, everyone in the village was talking about Artur's engagement breaking up, giving it a bad name that stretched like a straw tail from Clara's garden to the square. The straw mat with which some boys and girls had covered the ground signified that their courtship was over[6]. Meanwhile, Maria Clara was doing penance for her flightiness. She was completely demoralized and repentant, and convinced that their courtship, which had been meant to end in marriage, was over. During the hours that she spent thinking, the light of hope did not quite go out, however, because no one could be certain that her inconsequential adventure had put her chastity in peril. So, she began to make herself look prettier, changing her hairstyle so that it did not always look the same, changing it from straight to wavy, with a lock of hair falling over her eyes, and wearing blouses and skirts that Artur liked. When she went to Inês's shop she walked past his shop, glancing inside and being happy to see the young man's dark profile. And from the depths of her wounded heart, which was plunged into infinite sadness, came a lacerating nostalgia for the evenings when there was a novena and they would go up the path from Achada, hand in hand, blessing the church because it would unite them forever and it also allowed them to enjoy wandering along together almost every evening.

Sitting on his three-legged stool, Artur was not sure that it was Maria Clara who was being talked about because he had no more news of her. The uncertainty as to whether it was she or not disconcerted him. She could be innocent. After turning over these contradictory ideas, his conscience prompted him to go to his fiancée's house and sort it all out. The gossip mortified him, but the most annoying thing was that all the family in Achada was convinced that there were reasons for their engagement being over. He had a duty to himself and his fiancée to proceed cautiously. He needed to see her one night. And seeing her more than once looking anxiously in through the shop door as she passed by, he felt an urge

---

[6] Translator's note: It was the custom in Madeira to put a straw mat outside the front door to show that an engagement had ended.

to go out and talk to her and then accompany her back to Achada as he used to.

If he had not felt that his pride was hurt and that he was wounded to the depths of his soul, which continued to be held captive by the misfortune that had befallen him, he would have done so. While the silence of the street and the shop were allowing him to have these disquieting thoughts, Artur mechanically mended some patent leather shoes, following the habits of years as an apprentice and then a craftsman in the art of shoe making. But his attention was diverted from dwelling on his love life by Hilário's walking in. His beard had grown and he was wearing a cape over his broad mountain dweller's shoulders and cream leather work boots. His features showed he was in good health; his skin was swarthy and his shining eyes revealed his happiness. He was one of Artur's best customers. Every month he had his children's boots mended with heavy soles or their shoes with rubber soles. Artur was always delighted when Hilário came in the shop door because it meant that there was work. He never came into the shop except to ask for something to be done. Since he had come in now with his hands in his pockets, it must be for new shoes.

"Good afternoon, master cobbler!"

"It's been a long time since I saw you!"

"That's true. I've had my head in the clouds!"

"Business, eh?"

"Yes, big business. I've come to ask you to make three pairs of black shoes for my children. I need them by next weekend."

"Are you going to ship out or what?"

"I'm off. To Venezuela. You can't get on here. The land only gives you enough to eat, and barely enough to buy clothes. But anyone who buys and sells cattle doesn't do badly."

"So the shop doesn't make enough?"

"The credit gives me a headache. I've already transferred the lease. I'm going to try a new life."

Artur could not find anything to say in reply and remained silent.

"So, have everything ready by next week. Here are the measurements. Good afternoon."

After he had gone, Artur sat thinking about Hilário's decision to emigrate. He thought it was true that, although there wasn't much money and he wouldn't have enough capital to build a two-storey house with eight small rooms for one or two more years, he always saved two hundred escudos at the end of the month, when the business did well. But it was a hard life and was more hazardous than Hilário's. The proof was that next day at dawn he was going to walk over to Faial to buy a cow. This was a life that would kill anyone before his time. And if he married, the family would go on increasing as that was the law of life. With this idea racing through his mind, he closed the shop door thinking about travelling.

He went to bed early. His mother prepared a snack for him for the morning, a pork sandwich and a cup of coffee. Worried about making an early start next day when the sun came in through the window, thoughts of Clara stayed away from his mind. All the blessed night he dreamed about the good business deal that he hoped to make.

The red rays of the sun stained the glass in the window. He got up, put on his trousers and went to the stream to wash his face. In a few minutes, he was ready for the day ahead. He went out and closed the door. But he had to open it again as he had left his walking staff in the kitchen.

He went past the shop but continued without stopping, along the banks of the stream in the direction of São Cristóvão. The Porco had almost disappeared. Its water did not even have the strength to flow over the stones. Digging his walking staff into the rough ground of the Entrosa path, he reached the last steep turn, where the lonely dirt track turned left and continued down along a smoothly angled narrow section and then a straight section, and arrived at the first houses in Arco de São Jorge. Then, with the end of his stick knocking chips off the stones, the sweat rolling down his face and with no one to talk to, he climbed up to Arco Pequeno, which was half way up, but still a long way from Pedra Funda. There, when he was taking a shortcut through some pine trees, he met another traveller, a woman not yet thirty with a shawl around her shoulders. They struck up a conversation.

"Are you going far, sir?"

"To Faial."

"I'm going that way too!"

"Have you come far?"

"From Boaventura."

"So, we can keep each other company."

And so, talking together, they did not notice how hard the walk was or how long the ascents and descents were.

"Life is very hard, you know! Every week I take this same path because of the skimmed milk. I'm the one who keeps the tally of the milk.

"Here in the north, you can't earn what you can in the south, in the city. This is a small island. Those who don't have large farms only earn enough to eat what the land provides them with and not to go around stark naked."

"That's true. Do you see this skirt?" Lifting the hem of her skirt, Artur could see how white her legs were.

Understanding his mischievous glance, she exclaimed, "These already made more than one man lose his head!"

"Well, God bless them then!"

"But, as I was telling you, I still owe the peddler for this skirt. There are so many expenses! I have to pay for everything at home, you know!"

And the conversation drifted off into saucy anecdotes. From time to time, on the narrower bends, her full hips touched his leg. On top of the Rocha do Cortado, in a grassy dip turned yellow by the sun that tempted one to take a nap, she said to Artur, with a dreamy look in her eyes, "What if we stopped here for a bit of a rest?"

They sat down, crushing the dense grass. The way she sat made her skirt ride up.

"It's so nice to be here with you!"

And, after some minutes had passed, she murmured, "Not so hard, eh!"

When they said goodbye at the start of the Cruzinhas path, the expression that rose on the air was the one used for a casual meeting:

"Have a safe journey!"

***

The Sousa family in Cruzinhas was famous all along the north coast for being rich from cattle dealing. In the Faial area, where the autumn and winter snow clung to the ground and the abundant rain swelled the rivers, there was no shortage of grass and the animals never went hungry. So, Artur bought a young cow with brown patches on her flanks. He did his calculations: after selling the meat and sending the skin to be tanned, he could make eight hundred escudos.

Before returning home, so as to not spend the night on the road, he slept in one of the Sousas' houses where the windows looked out over a wide valley, the fences along the terraces and the river that dried up in summer. The bright light of the full moon spilled onto the floor. He remembered the woman with the shawl around her shoulders on the dry grass. And he thought and thought... Something in the moonlight had brought back the memory of the woman from Arco! The solution came to him: the moonlight made him see the yellowish grass because the light of the full moon over the Faial peaks was yellow too. He looked out of the window at the Cortado Mountain and his desire was for a sight of that dry grass. He tried to remember his casual companion's entire body. Without wanting it to, his image of Clara seemed to be dimmer, indistinct, although one persistent memory stayed with him: the fair on Sta. Quitéria's day, when their courtship started. But then, as this delightful picture was fading, the face of a man rose before his eyes, the image of the suspected traitor. He was overwhelmed by sadness and could no longer see the yellow grass, only the room, the bed, a pine chair and a staff painted red leaning in the corner, opposite the sofa. He brought his thoughts back to real life: this deal should be one of his most profitable.

***

Two months went by. He rarely left the shop to buy or sell cows. He was so used to working that when he did leave and was not sitting on his three legged stool working, he missed it. Even if it was only half an hour, it was enough to make him happy. There was no one better than Artur at the art of soling boots and finishing them off. So, customers flocked to him from villages near and far.

One evening in the week after he came back from Faial, he caught Maria Clara looking into the shop and he had the same feeling of curiosity that he had had the time before. He could not resist the urge to go out and meet her. He put down the wax that he was using on the thread for sewing the local administrator's shoes on the edge of table, closed the door and hurried after her, like a nanny goat behind its owner. She was half way down the road when she turned her head, as if she sensed him following her.

"Maria Clara!"

"Is it you, Artur? You didn't come back."

"So you don't know what you did? Didn't you give me up for someone else?"

"No. I'd never exchange you for someone else."

He was much calmer than during the days following that nocturnal encounter and he therefore told Maria Clara in detail how he had followed the lad and how he'd run him off that night. And if Artur had been incautious, it was because he was afraid that his revenge could lead to unfortunate consequences. She confessed that she was guilty and was sorry for not having been frank with him, even though being sincere could lead to her irremediable disgrace. When the story was over, she said:

"Now you know everything. Do what you want. I'm still the same. I like you."

Artur did not reply. They carried on walking until, as they were entering Achada, he said:

"We won't talk about what happened any more." And they went their separate ways at the entrance to Inês's yard.

***

Now, every morning, as autumn was painting the leaves on the trees burnt umber and nature was sadly remembering the season it had lived through, the two lovers bore witness to the truth, in the face of the false rumours and the meaningless gossip that had gone around. The news that Artur and Maria Clara would soon be getting married was already circulating among all the families in the area.

Like a prod piercing the skin of a sluggish animal, ambition was a goad that never stopped pushing Artur on to become rich. He began to raise the price of his shoes and his repairs. His customers began to go away, preferring a less expensive cobbler in Fajã do Penedo, despite the distance. The cattle business intensified, as it was more lucrative. But the sleepless nights spent thinking about who would buy the leather, who would pay better and how he could sell the meat tired him out and aged him, even though he was only a little over twenty. He would have to find another way to have better luck and make his life less harsh.

"I'm going to emigrate! I'm going to emigrate!" said Artur to himself, as he sat on his black linden wood three legged stool soling some cream leather work boots.

He could not get the letter from José de Abreu from Fajã de Penedo out of his mind. Adriano from Falca had showed him the letter. In it, Abreu said that Brazil was his new homeland. He had bought a farm three hours by train from the city of Rio de Janeiro. He regretted not having gone there sooner. There was no lack of cattle to raise and deal in and whatever you "*pranted*" grew in that soil.

Reading that letter was the catalyst for the intoxicating idea that stirred his spirit of adventure.

CHAPTER VII

The custom of putting the cattle into barns to fatten them up and produce milk comes from the earliest inhabitants of the Island. These barns are primitive huts with badly fitting stone walls, pine rafters and wheat straw roofs that perch on the hilltops or are built on the terraced slopes where crops grow all the year round. The animals are shut in day and night, rarely getting out, except to slake their thirst in the streams, ponds and rivers. They can be seen ambling along with their owner in front or behind, headed for the water where they can drink their fill. You can hear the sounds of the herd. Their noses touch the water and their mouths gulp it in for who knows how long, until their instinctive need has been satisfied. Then it's back to the barn, where they are tied to the manger.

Pimenta's wife and eldest son, with ropes on their shoulders and sickles in their hands, spent all the seasons of the year walking nimbly over the grassy slopes where the waterlogged folds in the ground had plenty of grass and other plants that the cattle could eat to provide tasty meat and rich, creamy milk. How often they would be caught in a downpour on the edge of the peaks that looked down on the winding rivers. Then they would lean against the trunks of the pine trees for shelter, hoping that the sheets of water would stop falling. One foggy autumn day, Alberto, Pimenta's son, was out cutting grass with a sickle when he slipped, tripped, rolled down the hillside and fell into the river gorge.

"Alberto, don't go over there. Go slowly; tread slowly."

"Don't worry, mother!"

His mother, for whom her son was the apple of her eye, wanted to break the fog apart to see where Alberto was. He moved away from her; about four metres away it was still possible to see the bushes. But suddenly it grew dark around them.

"Alberto? Alberto?"

Not even the voice of the fog, if it had been able to talk, could speak to her as it was so thick.

"Alberto? Alberto?"

She felt faint. She threw up her hands and clutched her head. Overcome, her eyes were bulging in their sockets and her reason fled. She could not take a single step in the gloom and with the fog taking away the strength of her legs she sat down. But anxiety, which is instinctive logic, took possession of her and she stood up and shouted and shouted. Only the fog heard her cries, it was so thick. Not even an echo of her anxious voice came back to her as the fog has no soul.

A lucid moment came into the agitated mind of the mother, who did not know what had happened to her son. She began to cry out in a voice made tearful by the pain in her maternal heart,:

"My son! My son!" But neither the breeze nor the trees replied.

"What is to become of me?"

And once more she lost all reason. She wrung her hands, clasping and unclasping her fingers. She lifted up her arms and in a fury began to tug at her hair, impulsively trying to pull it out. She sat down on the wet ground, hung her head and sobbed.

Meanwhile, the sun came out and dispersed the thick fog. The light shone on the slopes where Alberto had been walking. As if by a miracle, instinct guided the woman's footsteps. She ran over and looked down to see if her son was lying injured somewhere between the rocks.

"My son! My son!"

The light moved to the bottom of the cliff. From the top of the rocky peak, the mother scanned the slope that dropped precipitously into the winding ravine. There was no sign of life – or of death.

She turned back. Not knowing what had happened to him, her ignorant soul had been suffering to the point of death for love of her son. But then she calmed down. She thought that maybe he had gone farther on. Her hope was reborn. She took hold of the sickle and went to cut the grass that was growing here and there on the hillocks. Then she collected it into bundles and tied them up with the rope. Calmly, as if there was nothing on her mind, she went down the mountain paths. She seemed not to be suffering. Her mind was clouded.

That peaceful morning, she went down to the barn. She undid the bundle of grass. She put in the manger and spread it out. Then she went home. When she opened the door, and saw the black calfskin shoes that Alberto wore on Sundays, her memory was reawakened. She began wailing, her forehead creased, crying out for Sta. Quitéria to tell her where her son was. Her husband had gone to Arco to discuss the price of a calf. A neighbour ran quickly to where the voice was coming from.

"What's happened?"

"The fog killed my son!"

"Where?"

"On the slopes."

"Then he'll be at the bottom of the river bank." And he shouted repeatedly with all his might:

"Manel? Manel?"

"What is it, father?"

"Come here."

When the boy came, he sent him to Rufino's house, telling him to find him and not to dawdle.

Meanwhile, the little ones from the village crowded around the woman who was sobbing, "My poor son! Oh my son!"

Instead of sitting at the door, old Semiã came walking up with the little strength that was left to him after a lifetime spent among the brush covered mountains, leaning on a walking stick as his legs were losing their strength. He was about ninety years old and heard voices when no one was speaking to him.

"What happened" What is it? Is it Judgement Day?"

And they told him that Alberto, Pimenta's son, had fallen off the mountain side and landed at the bottom of the valley.

"What a tragedy! What a tragedy! Who knows if he is still alive?"

"Alive? Only if Sta. Quitéria performs a miracle," growled Inácia.

"A miracle!"

"So it's not possible?"

"Nah! How can he be alive if those rocks are almost at heaven's door!" broke in Jeremias's widow, a black scarf tied on her head.

"God's power is great, Maria Getrudes!"

While these comments were being made, Jacinto, the neighbour, his son and Rufino set off along the bed of the river, on the same level as the lower fields that bordered on the river bank.

"You know, thinking about it, Death is always around! But that way! Such a good boy!" commented Rufino.

"When you're feeding the cattle, you're always in danger," replied Jacinto.

"It's a hard life and you only get money that you can't save."

"Yes, only those who work with raising cows know what a struggle it is."

"Whoever is lucky enough to ship out is the one who can put by a bit of money."

"This collecting grass for the cows… jumping out of bed in rain and fog!"

"This place is bad. It's all rocks."

"Neighbour Pimenta does some deals, but it's not much of a business. The family goes for grass and the profit still doesn't stretch to buying the Rochão farm. How many years is it that he's been raising cattle and buying and selling?"

"It's a miserable life you live raising cattle and keeping cows."

"And the worst is, these disasters happen." Jacinto's son, who had gone on in front, curious to see where Alberto had fallen, ran back to his father and Rufino, who were walking in single file, to bring them the tragic news.

"Alberto has fallen flat on top of a rock in the river. His head is covered in blood."

They went another few hundred metres before they saw the sad spectacle. The unhappy boy was lying there, barefoot, with his shirt torn and his head covered in blood, with his eyes open and glazed over with the pained expression of death. The rocks rose up to the heavens with almost vertical sides and in the sliver of earth at the sides of the trickle of water grew creepers and arum lilies, whose white flowers adorned the place with a cold beauty and kept vigil over the place of death.

Rufino, whose muscles were hard, put the dead boy on his back and without a moment's rest went straight to the yard of the Pimenta's house, where the piercing cries of the women echoed as if it was Judgement Day.

Back from Arcos, Pimenta was distraught and on the verge of unbearable despair, exclaiming:

"I'm going to end it all! I'm going to end it all! I'm going to throw myself off that rock!" And start running, without thinking, towards the rocks.

Jacinto and Rufino followed him and calmed him down with encouraging words, making him see that his action would go against God's will and reminding him that life and death are inseparable.

Broken, Pimenta went back home and sat down on a bench, holding his son's hand in one of his.

Around the yard, comments were made about the accident.

"Those who work to live are bound to die!" said Cantoneiro.

"That's the law of life," said Inácio.

"Feeding cattle is worse than digging, watering, trapping, cutting down pine trees, carrying firewood on your back and dragging branches down from the mountains," said Lucas.

"That's the second person to fall off the rocks in two years," said Inácio's son.

The little village was sad as the pain had entered the souls of the whole community, where most of the families were related either by descent or marriage. They all felt the pain, without the hypocrisy of the words that people learn in urban areas, where they put on a sad expression but are indifferent in their hearts. The afternoon was one of mourning. The boys and girls of Alberto's age did not leave the Pimenta's cottage. They sadly remembered the games that they used to play on Sundays in Rufino's yard under the chestnut tree. Even Mariazinha, who had only met Alberto once at the Sta. Quitéria's day festival, came all the way from Levada to bring him a large wreath of white flowers, with the contrite expression of one who will never see him again around the parish.

CHAPTER VIII

Inês felt that she had been defeated in the fight to improve their financial situation. Her hope was withering away. She had been born with no material possessions, like her husband. Their life was a struggle, suffering, working hard on the land as their ancestors had done, following the same routine in order to scrape a living out of the soil, and the battle only gave them enough not to die of hunger. Where the soil was fertile, the wild strawberries grew so plump they looked as if they had been manufactured. But such a poor life only produced poor people. She went into the grocery business convinced that the shop would be her Promised Land.

One night, after they had done the accounts, the month's takings were 1,870 escudos. And more than half of this would not go into the cash drawer. The credit terrified them. Barbado from Falca alone owed them 2,000 escudos. His wife had been sick in bed, crippled, for over a year. Their five small children made their orders bigger and their beans, which had been attacked by blight, wouldn't fill half a dozen measures. And there were others like Barbado. Parruca from Ribeira do Minho had lost his footing when he was cutting some vines and rolled to the bottom of the cliff, getting stuck between the rocks. By some miracle, he did not hit his head but he did break both his legs. And turning the page full of figures that marched down the page, at the bottom of the fateful debtors' ledger she spotted the sum of 1,500 escudos for the current year, a sum of money that would never be paid. Ladeira had died and his cow, his only valuable possession, had been taken by Artur in payment for an old debt.

With sorrow eating at her heart, the pencil rolled off the table without her noticing and dropped onto a paraffin can with a clang. Superstitiously, Inês said to herself:

"Someone wants to talk to me."

She closed the book. Francisco was arranging empty boxes in one corner when a little body squeezed under the door. It was the biscuit mouse. He hit the mousetrap with a stick, a mousetrap that seemed to have human sensitivity as it never caught the mouse. The mouse belonged to the same class of animal as clever fish. Francisco called the biscuit mouse clever. It could see the bit of meat in the trap and smell it, but it never touched it or nibbled at it. On the shelf where they kept the macaroni puddings, there was a line of droppings. The mouse went that way when it was hungry. Francisco was furious but at the same time he felt a sense of justice contradicting his desire to kill the scoundrel: it had a right to live too like all mortals since it was only looking after itself in the shop. After piling up the boxes, he took the mousetrap and put it between the biscuit tin and the oil can, where there was a little hole in the lid and he could see inside. Near the opening there was a dead fly lying in the spilt oil.

While he was doing this, someone knocked on the door. Inês went to open it. Barefoot, with a short beard that was turning white and with his shirt front stained with dark patches from working hard up on the mountain, Barbado greeted her timidly, expecting not to be served.

"God give you a good night." And he went up to the counter. Since he did not say anything more, Inês asked him:

"Do you need something" The question and the tone in which it was asked encouraged Barbado to speak.

"I hate to buy things on credit but my luck is terrible. My wife can't move to pick up a straw off the floor. The kids are running around in the grass. The oldest goes up the mountain every day to get a bit of firewood so we can cook. Last year there were no beans. The hundred escudos I'd saved up were spent on my wife's illness. My son António wants to go to work at someone's house. If he gets a job, he'll have a bed, food and clothes and shoes. And then there are the others! My wife cries and bemoans her bad luck. Potatoes and cabbage don't cost anything but when you're ill you feel like eating something better. So, I came to buy some bread and a tin of tuna."

Inês was upset by the tale of misfortune. She went to the shelf, took down a loaf of bread and a tin of tuna and wrapped them in piece of brown paper. As she was gong to hand them over, a sudden thought made her stop. She went back to the shelf, took down a packet of macaroni and gave it to Barbado.

"Take this to make some soup for that sick woman!" He stammered out his thanks for her kindness and went out.

Inês stood still with a feeling of relief in her heart. There were those who had many needs and no one to help them, pushed by destiny and without any strength to fight it. There was she, struggling against the destiny that had been handed down by her ancestors over many generations; the people of Achada had always lived and died in poverty. She was the first person in that place to react against what had always been. She was swimming against the current of the past and the present; it reminded her of the water in the river that flowed down from the mountain to the sea all year round. But that was what happened to the river: unlike people, it could not go back. People followed the path that their minds dictated. It was a charitable gesture on her part to give to someone who had nothing but had not begged. Barbado, who was poor enough to beg, deserved that much. She looked at what she had given him and, comparing him with many others, she accepted it sadly. She would never see the money, of course, but she had treated the man in a friendly manner and talked to him and served him, giving him more credit, everything on credit.

After going over the debtor's ledger, Inês and her husband decided on the spot, after Barbado had left, that their lives had to take another course. She said to Francisco:

"The big prize in the lottery only goes to someone who buys a ticket. We have our lottery ticket in our hands. We can win. Luck depends on determination. Let's let others say that it was luck that was responsible!"

Time did not stand still. The months passed. The fields around Achada changed and marked the passage of time with the changing colour of the vegetation, the shading of the wild plants, the appearance of the fields and even the flowers that grew more profusely during one season than during another, such as groundsel and balsam. Kilting up their skirts, the women helped the men to dig the ground, make irrigation channels and sow the seeds. They repeated the age-old actions that had petrified into a routine. These habits belonged to all those living on the island, whether on the mountain sides or on the coast. Even their archaic language, with expressions that dated back five hundred years, belonged to the human beehive in all its social and individual rusticity.

***

In September, Inês received an invitation to go and spend a few days in the city with Maria Matilde, the godmother of one of Inês's daughters. She was the daughter of one of the shops' suppliers and lived in old Rua das Pretas, almost at the end. From the upstairs bay window, the door of the church of St. Peter was visible.

On a misty autumn morning, the tops of the hills and the gorges of the Torrinhas mountains were thickly shrouded in fog. Like dusty layers of drifting ash, bands of fog floated on the wind from the southwest. Their staffs clinking on the stones of the steep paths, Inês and her daughter climbed peaks covered in heather that had been beaten down by the wind and then plunged down into leafy woods of holly, laurel and privet, as if they had gone back in time and were part of the first wave of colonists. Climbing slowly and with difficulty, it was only a fear of witches that scared them. The rustling of wild boar among the bushes presaged something bad. Carolina moved the umbrella that she was carrying to her left hand and her mother moved the bag of yams that she was holding by the string to her other hand so that they could cross themselves. While they walked on and on, thoughts ran unceasingly through Inês's head, and the agitation of her ideas was like a pot of boiling water.

Sometimes a flurry of ideas ran into each other, sometimes one idea overwhelmed the rest and then immediately flowed into a string of other ideas: the shop and its business, in which she had put her trust, the ruin that faced them because of the debts. If the merchandise would only go out of the door in exchange for money, then life would change and she could achieve her dreams. But who bought with money? Those customers could be counted on one hand. No, no, it was impossible. The shop was running into debt because its income did not cover the expenses. They had to change their quality of life. Her husband was a persistent man, who would take on any kind of work and succeed. By adding the little bits together, a little could become a lot. But out of the little bits, she needed to take what was needed to pay for the family's expenses and with the rest she scrimped and saved. How many years would it take to have enough for a comfortable life? They would never become the most important couple in Achada do Castanheiro. Thinking these thoughts, the way seemed short and the time passed in her mind, not according to the sun. So, they came down the track from the Torrinhas and went up the endless twists and turns by Curral. When they saw the city, the light streaming down from the sky was already pale.

Night was falling as they walked down the cobblestones of Pico Street. Inês looked at the church of St. Peter, saw that the door was open and crossed herself. At the end of Rua das Pretas, an oxcart with two foreigners stopped in front of the Felisberta cake shop. The window was lit up and on the stands the yellow teardrop shapes of egg yolk sweets and the plates with various kinds of cakes made Inês' and her daughter's mouths water. As they came closer, their appetites were awakened by the sight. The journey on foot had used up their energy and pangs of hunger came over them. Godmother was waiting for them, of course, but those cakes were not sold at the feast of Sta. Quitéria and a cake would taste good before dinner. They went in. At a little round table on which there was a plate with a blue painted border containing several pastries, sat a young woman with her legs crossed so that the milky white of her thigh could be seen. Inês was struck by her lack of shame. For her, the idea of womanly virtue was bodily modesty in the face of the sin of lechery, which was how one lived according to the rules of antiquated village morality, and that woman had lost her modesty. She lost her confused look when the shop assistant asked her if she wanted something. Each of them ordered a very fancy looking cake. When they left the shop, Inês could not resist looking out of her eye corner at the crossed legs of that brazen girl.

***

The knocker jangled and the door opened. They climbed the stairs to where Matilde was waiting at the top.

"You must be tired!"

"Our legs held up well to the journey."

"Come in, come in! The food is on the table."

And they talked about life, how different it was in Achada and in the city. There, people lived surrounded by the mountains and the hedges of the farms, sowing and reaping. Here, people lived in houses that crowded cheek by jowl with only the streets to separate them, and the work was done with somewhere to shelter from the bad weather. There, there was no light at night on the roads, the sky and the paths were dark, the moon and stars were hidden by clouds. Here, the shop windows seemed to have the light of day in them and the street lighting made the streets look gay. Inês did not feel unlucky to have been born and raised far from the city, but she did confess to her friend that she would like to have more comforts in the house, without her family going short of anything, and wearing clothes and shoes that were better than they could buy in the country. And to come to the city on the bus every month to enjoy in her own way the things that did not exist in Achada do Castanheiro. It was while they were talking that she opened up and told Matilde of her wish: to emigrate to Venezuela. Her husband would go first and when it was possible, she and the children would follow him. Matilde listened and agreed with the ideas that bubbled in Inês's head. She thought her desire to improve their lives was normal and told Inês about the problems that she had had when her husband, who was the cashier in an ironmonger's, hardly earned enough for such a small family's needs; there was only the wife and their daughter was still small at that time. But luck did not abandon them: an agent from an agricultural company in Antigua came to Funchal to take back a few dozen young men who wanted to find employment in various kinds of jobs. They met the requirements. It was still an adventure as they were emigrating to an unknown land. Matilde had intended to follow her husband. But her doubts as to whether she could stand the climate made her give up the idea. The world had now gone round the sun four times and she had a reasonable amount of savings in the bank. To leave one's homeland without having the means to win the fight with those who want everything for themselves, those with the blind egotism of someone who takes no notice of others, casts a shadow over one's happiness, if we can ever really be happy.

Inês told in detail of the ways she had tried not to be separated from her husband and to live in blissful harmony in the backwater of Achada. As she talked, she stole a glance at a corner of the dining room where a box glimmered with gold; at the glasses of various sizes ranged on the glass fronted shelves of a large dresser that stood against the wall; at another cupboard where a black and white marble stand held two glass vases. In the middle of the other wall hung a picture in which oranges, apples and bananas were arranged in a bottle green bowl, painted with such perfect realism that Inês's daughter ingenuously asked if those were real oranges on the tray.

The small guest room with a window looking out on the narrow garden behind the houses held a bed made of good chestnut wood. Visitors from the country slept in there. Inês found it hard to go to sleep. Her mind was in turmoil. The idea that her Francisco could go seek his fortune like Matilde's husband left her restless and sleepless for hours. In her mind, she made her cherished idea come true: a modern house in Achada do Castanheiro. She fell asleep in the end, while her daughter breathed as peacefully as if she had been at home in her own uncomfortable room.

When morning came, its rosy colours proclaiming the modesty of nature in wearing a silken nightgown, Inês peeked out between the slats of the shutters and was shocked to see a stunted fig tree that seemed to want to free itself from the well formed by the walls of the houses. What they called a garden was little more than a well. And she said to herself, "Poor fig tree! It can't even stretch out its arms!"

She remembered the huge fig tree in Cabo da Ribeira that sprouted and grew just as it wanted to, in a field that was large enough for its branches to spread out. She opened the shutters, put her head out and looked at the sky. All she could see was a patch of blue. Depressed, she felt homesick for the great globe of the sky on top of the mountain in Achada. And she imagined a new house with a veranda, built on their land with the money that Francisco would earn over there in Venezuela.

Lunch was taken up, from start to finish, with talking about going abroad. Matilde mentioned several emigrants, some of whom she knew because they were relatives, and others that she had been told about.

"You know, Inês, those who've gone away are now rich."

"If only I could! People from the city are smarter than country folk! I know very well that my husband is not one of the lazy ones."

And as she talked, her eyes moved surreptitiously over the fine china plates with a pattern of trees and the knives and forks that looked as if they were made of silver. Carolina looked taken aback as she stared and stared again at the oil paintings hanging on the wall and the red velvet curtain hiding the door. But what most surprised her was the parrot in the kitchen doorway, with feathers in colours that she had never seen before.

Her astonishment was only natural. It was because there were such things to see that her curiosity was like that of the marmalade cat that jumped up from the wooden floor onto a chair. Carolina did not know whether what her eyes were seeing was like what the cat saw, even if her teacher had said that animals have eyes, but what people see should not be confused with what a goat or a dog sees. She still lacked the reasoning to ask herself whether the cat could see the colours of the parrot's feathers or whether this was reserved for people, and why.

They went out after Raquel went to school. They walked down Rua das Pretas looking into the shop windows. Carolina's eye was caught by the blouses with red spots, the well cut skirts, the belts with gilt buckles, the big handbags to put your prayer book and rosary in. She felt an urge to dress like the girls who were walking by. Her eyes wanted everything, just as her mouth had watered and she had felt hungry for the cakes that she had seen for the first time at the Felisberta cake shop. She was in the city. The sound of the church bells sounded different from the ones in the church back home. What a contrast between Achada and Rua das Pretas. Inês did not feel as perturbed as her daughter because, while the girl was overwhelmed by the outward appearance of what she saw, drinking it in like a leach and committing it to memory, her mother was concentrating on one thought that dominated all others, even while she was listening to Matilde, her daughter's godmother: the idea of emigrating and becoming rich. She didn't want a string of buildings like those on Rua da Carreira; she wanted a two storey house.

They continued walking to the Bazar do Povo, a big department store, and went in. At the counters, people of all ages were elbowing each other aside. The newcomers focused on the women dressed in silk and wearing patent leather shoes, with jewelled rings and fancy handbags. But what surprised them most was to see above their heads, just below the ceiling, two wires on which little boxes travelled, boxes of money which an employee seated on a tiny throne received so that she could send back the change. The wires criss-crossed the store to the various departments.

Inês and her daughter looked in amazement at what looked to them like a toy. They went round the ground floor and the first floor. Inês looked at a sewing machine. While she was thinking about buying it, the idea of emigrating rose from the depths of her memory and she said to the assistant:

"I can't make a decision now."

"But madam is so interested in it! I can offer you easy payments."

"No, sir. My life is not settled."

Meanwhile, the assistant showed her another machine, a bigger one with a shinier lid. Inês's eyes were drawn to it. But the idea of emigrating overcame the desire to own it, although she needed to do her sewing at home so as not to have to depend on favours from Leonarda in Serrão. And then there was the time spent going there.

In the midst of all this, Matilde commented:

"Don't worry, Mr. Luís. If my friend ever buys a machine, she'll only come here."

They went out of the door that opens on to the river. The sight of the festoons of bougainvillea that cover it and the profusion of flowers in an orgy of green and red was not lost on Inês, who bent over the wall to get closer to them. She looked between the clusters of flowers and could not see a drop of water. How could this canal with its high walls be called a river when there wasn't a drop of water? Up in Achada, the Minho, where there was always water flowing summer and winter, now that was a river. She thought this to herself, but she did not reveal her thoughts to her friend. They called it a river and she wouldn't be the one to change its name. Yes, a little woman who lived up in the mountains of Boaventura giving herself airs just because she had been to school up to the fourth year; that would give her *comadre* something to laugh about. The godmother and goddaughter, who were engrossed in looking at the crockery in the window of the department store, tore themselves away, went over to Inês and strolled on idly in the gentle warmth of the afternoon.

As they were turning the corner from Travessa do Forno into Rua dos Ferreiros, someone said:

"Good afternoon, Mrs. Matilde! I can see that you're well. I'm doing well too."

"I wasn't expecting to see you."

"Why?"

"Weren't you going to join your husband?"

"That's next month. Such a long journey is going to be hard."

"So your husband has gone away?" asked Inês.

"Yes indeed. He's been in Venezuela for three years and God has been good to him. But a woman wants to be with her man."

"You're right. Out of sight… There are women who want men's very marrow. Imagine, a hussy stole the husband of a woman in Achada. And she was unmarried and pure."

"You know, it's not surprising. The world has always been like that."

"Goodbye, Mrs. Matilde." And to her two companions, "Bye bye."

They turned into Rua dos Ferreiros. An ox cart came down it with its curtains covered in dust. The roadway was steaming from the droppings of the animals. Attracted by the novelties in the shop windows, Inês and Carolina pressed up to them, wanting to see the things close to and with their hands held out as if to grab them. Carolina pointed to a red satin blouse.

They walked on, quickening their steps to cross the Largo do Colégio. The pigeons, some pecking at the maize spread out over the ground and others swallowing it hungrily, were used to the passers by and took no notice of the intrusion.

Slowly, they walked back to Rua das Pretas.

CHAPTER IX

Artur and Maria Clara got married. That morning, the local people, wearing either their Sunday best or their everyday clothes, went to the church as if it were the eve of their patron saint's day. After the ceremony, the curious from the area around and the neighbours from Achada made two lines and threw flowers at the newly weds. And, near the house, by the door, was Ratazana's son, who had made an arch out of two curved sticks and decorated it with smilax, mimosa, lilies and wild ginger from the river bank. When they got back from church, the couple was surprised to hear the sound of a harmonica and ukulele played by Artur's godsons, who had come from Arco to celebrate their godfather's wedding and thank him for his generosity. At Easter he had given each of them a pair of leather boots.

The years passed by, taking with them the months and people's lives, from the moment when dawn came until the night called the people back to their cottages, while Artur spent more time dealing in cattle than mending shoes.

He ordered shoes from the city that had been manufactured in Porto. They sold better than handmade ones; for a year now his customers had bought them because they said they lasted longer. But dealing in leather, the money came in like handfuls of maize, not three or four grains a day. But one way or another, it only gave him enough to get by, to eat and buy clothes.

One night after he had gone home from the cobbler's shop and had dinner, while his two children were playing on the kitchen floor with the cardboard cars that their godparents had given them for Christmas, Artur unburdened himself to his wife.

"One day we'll have another child. I earn the same money but the expenses keep on going up. Why don't I try my luck and go to Brazil? It'll be hard to leave you and the children, and the house...

but the money we earn in the village means we'll always be poor. Last week when I was in Arco, I heard that Gonçalves from Quebrada, who went to São Paulo in Brazil eight years ago, had sent back so much money to the family that their new house can be seen from the road and it's the biggest and the best in the parish. I don't have all the money for the trip but I can ask for the rest."

"It will be hard for me too to stay here with the children. I know I have my mother and father nearby… But we got married never to be separated, didn't we?"

"In a few years I hope to God that I can send for you and the children." And, after a moment's silence, "I heard that it won't be long before Manuel Carvalhosa emigrates. And the shop must be a good business."

"A good business! What about the credit? It's even worse than being a shoemaker."

Next day, the rosy-cheeked sun crept into Artur's bedroom through the cracks in the shutters.

It gave him renewed energy. He got out of bed without waking Maria Clara, captivated by the idea of changing their lives. He had to go to Brazil. He would try his luck. When his wife came into the kitchen, he told her that he had decided to go to the city. He would be back next day.

He took the usual route, walking over the Torrinhas. He got his passport with the help of policeman, who was a relative. He booked his passage at the shipping agency for the end of May and went back to Achada as happy as the day he got married. Maria Clara showed the sadness that she felt at their uncertain future. If he was robbed or killed, or if an illness carried him off, what would become of her and the children!

He needed 70,000 escudos to invest in the first deal. Who would lend him that amount of money? But it had to happen. The boat would arrive in Funchal on the 30th. Then he remembered that Mr. Adriano from Falca had loaned him three thousand for a cattle deal that he had made two years before. He marched off swinging his arms along the winding trail along the river bank that sometimes was steep and sometimes hardly rose or fell, heading directly to Falca. The elderly Adriano was sitting on a three legged stool at the door of his house, sunning himself in the bright sun on a morning that smelt of the flowers and wild plants that encircled the yard like a crown.

"What brings you to these parts, Mr. Artur? Sit down on the bench."

The conversation soon drifted away from the main point. They talked about breeding cattle, about cows that gave plenty of good milk, about calves that were not fed properly and about the pigs that would be killed for Christmas. When this topic had been exhausted, Artur, feeling slightly embarrassed, asked for a loan of 70.000 escudos. When the conditions for the loan had been settled, he returned to Achada. He took up his guitar and played and sang *fados* as he had when he was a bachelor and winked at the girls at the festivals for Senhor Bom Jesus and St. Brás.

PART TWO

THE EMIGRANT

CHAPTER X

The *Cape Horn*[7], a Spanish emigrant boat, rode at anchor near the city docks. It was a clear evening in May, with an opalescent sky that stretched to the curve of the horizon. As if in a circus, but one with no ropes, the sharp eyed seagulls did acrobatics over the water around the steamer, circling in search of scraps of food.

Artur went down the steps of the quay and jumped into the launch, which was already full of passengers. It left the steps where the water lapped and slowly puffed its way toward the ship, cleaving through Neptune's domain. The foreign women chattered while they tried to keep their traditional straw hats on their heads and with the other hand tried to grab hold of the rope on the steep gangway of the ship. Artur went looking for his trunk among the mountains of luggage. Discouraged, he thought it had been stolen because of its cow skin cover, held in place by yellow headed nails. Just when he had given up looking for it, his trunk turned up under a hatch cover.

The *Cape Horn* set sail under a starry sky. After the passengers in tourist class had had dinner, they went up on deck. The lights of the city shimmered in the distance and a light breeze was blowing. Those who had hired deck chairs were dozing in them. The rest preferred to go into the saloon to dance or to talk. Sitting on a bench next to two Italian girls, a young man was playing the harmonica. The sad sounds of folk music filled the room. Artur was infected by the sadness of the melody and felt homesick for Achada and his family. Then he noticed that a pretty girl was looking at him. The sadness left him. He went to his trunk and got his guitar. He tuned it from the harmonica and began to sing along with the dreamy music. The girl, who had brown eyes and a dark skin, joined the group. She must have been about 25 years old. She was from Czechoslovakia but she had lived in Rome with her parents since she was a child

---

[7] «Cabo Hornos» in the original

because her mother, who was a Roman, was a partner in a hairdressing salon. The other partner had taken over the salon as if by magic. They became poor. Meanwhile, she had married an Italian who had gone to São Paulo. She had left her parents in Rome working in a hat factory. Now she was going to join her husband. She was wearing a dark red blouse and the chestnut brown hair encircling her head gave her a graceful air that set her apart from the other emigrants.

With one elbow on the edge of the bar, a man from Madeira was arguing and joking with another man and making faces.

"What's that face for?"

"That's how that Jew frowned when he talked to me."

"But he was right, in part. The goat was yours but the brambles were his."

"How can that be? The stream starts in the mountains and there are no boundaries in the mountains."

"Look, doesn't he have more land than you?"

"That's true. But that bluff is mine. Is that the only way to get on? To have kindling for the fire? No. That's why I'm going to Brazil. Twenty-one of us from Campanário have left our families and our land."

"Those who have the most are always on top. The laws weren't made for people who only live on a few fields of potatoes. I'm going to try my luck out there too. If all goes well, with the money I make, I'll have a house built on my father's bit of land. There's nothing like your own place. My eyes filled with tears the size of berries when I looked back and Campanário was lost in the dark…"

"Listen to that music…It's like being at the feast of St. Bras!"

And the two of them went to join the group. The one from Campanário, who had a clumsy body, stuck his hands in his pockets and, as he was taller than his compatriot, stood behind him so that they could both see the musicians. Artur felt an arm touch his. He turned his head and saw that the Czech girl was leaning against him in the opening in the circle.

Since they were all, or almost all, from the provinces and a life that sprang from nature, so that the first sounds they had heard had been the wind whistling in the branches of the trees on stormy nights and the ballads that accompanied the work in the fields and the pilgrimages, all the spectators were fascinated by the melancholy notes that reminded them of their carefree childhood.

Afterwards, the young Iberians and Italians danced to the sleepy notes of the tango. Then again the harmonica played archaic-sounding popular music, weeping out over the saloon like water bubbling out of a rocky crevice. They could hear the uproar of the voices of the families sitting on the side benches opposite the bar. Those most in need of the freshness of the beer did not stray far. At a corner table, a card game was being played. And in the stern near the bulkhead was a couple of newly weds looking at the sea dreamily under the stars, enjoying the romantic pleasures of life, unaware that the memory records the fleeting moments of internal time and that the calendar inexorably marks the passage of external time. Little by little the party broke up and one by one they left the saloon till it was as empty as the desert, where there are as many mysteries as there are humans who come from Adam's rib.

CHAPTER XI

The days lengthened. The heat was like an oven. And the further the ship sailed toward the place where day and night are equal, the more the emigrants complained that they could not sleep in their bunks. Finally, they abandoned them and lay down in the deck chairs that were scattered about the upper deck.

Late one night, when the temperature was even higher than before, Artur was wandering between the deck chairs. He was looking around to see if he could find the Czech girl, because he was attracted to her body as if she had a positive electrical charge and he a negative one. He stopped by an empty chair and as the heat was bothering him and the owner was not around, he sat down. The chair skidded and hit the leg of the Czech girl, who opened her eyes.

"I'm sorry, I didn't mean to!"

He did not understand what she said to him in a language that sounded like Spanish. But he remembered a few words and phrases in Spanish that the parish priest had taught him and concluded that Italian was similar to how people speak in Spain.

It was a very hot night. The sound of the waves hitting the side of the ship and splashing up whirls of foam could hardly be heard. The engines, as they pushed the ship though the southern seas like a plough, sounded an enormous panting beast.

The deckchairs where the Czech girl and Artur were drowsing were in the dark triangle formed by a companionway, out of the light of the lamp, halfway along from the stern. A sudden rocking interrupted their drowsiness and made her open her eyes. Turning her head, she said, "*Sta bene?*"

Artur glanced at her and did not know what to reply. He had only heard the "sta".

She repeated the words and he understood the question.

"I'm fine."

In the heat of the equatorial night, the blood pulsated, with an ardent, siren song that called out for free, instinctive sex and not fraternal feelings. In the enveloping heat of the night, with the smell of the sea, the two of them exchanged only a few brief words.

Next day, the deck chairs did not remain empty after dinner. Odd words very often remained in Artur's head, waiting for a reply that he could not give because he did not understand.

"*Caldo,*" she said. And he thought that the soup at lunch had been good. But what the Czech girl was trying to say was that the weather was hot. And because touch spoke more eloquently than words, one night she took hold of his hands with her white hands with the slim fingers. Silently, in the patch of darkness, love was developing. Two emigrants in shirt sleeves passed by, but they did not look into the patch of darkness.

"Brazil is a gold mine! I've been living in Belo Horizonte for seven years and I can tell you that I'm rich. I have four grocer's shops. I went back to Portugal to spend a month with my parents and now I'm going back."

"This is my first time. I'm going to try my luck. I'm young."

"Where are you from?"

"From Minho."

And they went away, down the companionway with the dark blue painted handrail that led to the smoking room.

The dull noise of the engines could be heard in the silence on deck. The Czech girl squeezed Artur's hands tightly, stood up and sat on his knee. The night sky was clear and full of stars and the Southern Cross was glimmering.

After a few, slow days, when the sea also rose and fell slowly, a shape could be seen in the distance. It grew more and more solid and came closer to the surface of the water. It was reality and did not come from the imagination, but it seemed that it did not really exist and was only images created by the mind and reflected in the eyes because they had spent so long out of sight of land. If it had not been for the entrance, the Guanabara Bay would have been a lake with green banks. The calmness of the sea was like that of a lake. Palm trees and other tropical trees with leafy green tops stood out above the bay. From the first class deck, the passengers gazed in fascination at what they had never seen before and their thoughts wandered. Their memories went back in time, to the time when the chronicler of the discoveries[8] gave his impression of the local people: *"there were three or four sweet damsels there with long, very black hair hanging down their backs and their unmentionables so high and so shameless..."*

The ship tied up to the quay. There was a confusion of trunks and baskets and of people anxious to get onto the land that made the deck look like Judgement Day, as if it had been turned into a market when the stalls are taken down at the end of the day and a noisy crowd of customers suddenly rushes in. Artur picked up his companion's luggage and took it to Customs. Then he went to find his own trunk, which had remained on deck. After completing the entry formalities and sending on their luggage, they got into a taxi.

"Where to?"

"The station, for the train for São Paulo," Artur replied.

The taxi went down the long streets, some less busy than others where the traffic took time to sort itself out, until the station loomed before their eyes. The Czech girl got out and gave Artur a card with her address in São Paulo: Elda Lamanna, Avenida Barão do Rio Branco, 1680.

"Domani avere São Paulo," Artur said to her as they said goodbye.

Then, after opening his wallet and reading the address written on the back of an envelope, he said to the driver, "Rua Senador Vergueiro, 37."

It was on that street in the city of Rio de Janeiro that a man from Funchal lived who had bought hides from him and to whom he had been sent with recommendations. The taxi stopped.

"How much do I owe you?"

"Are you Portuguese? I know that from the way you speak. You don't pay anything. I'm homesick for Portugal... for my land ... Good luck!"

"Then let's go and have a drink!"

---

[8] Translator's note: An extract from the letter written in 1500 by the chronicler Pero Vaz de Caminha to King Manuel of Portugal about Pedro Alvarez de Cabral's voyage of discovery.

"It'll have to be another time. And in case you need it, here's my name and my address," he said, giving Artur a card, which had a picture of the car on it.

Artur went into the "bar". António Silva, a tall, burly man of over forty, was at the counter, taking two cruzeiros from a customer, when, to his surprise, he recognised his fellow countryman. After talking to Artur about life on the Island, he insisted that he spend that night at his house.

Next day, Artur, who had not forgotten Elda, took the train to São Paulo. Even though there was a strong wind that night, it was very hot. He had slept badly because of the long trip and the swaying of the train. When it stopped, he left the station and took a taxi to Avenida Barão do Rio Branco.

Because he did not know about lifts, he mountaineered his way up the stairs to the seventh floor. He looked at the door post, found the bell, pushed the button with his thumb and listened carefully to hear the metallic ring. Several seconds went by. The door opened and, as if a very bright light had suddenly blinded him, Artur was amazed to see a beautiful woman in a robe, who looked very different from the girl he had met on the ship.

"Come in," she said in Italian. "My husband left me a letter to say that he has gone to Minas Gerais on business."

After closing the door, Elda put her arm around his waist and snuggled up to him. Passively, he let himself be taken into her room, where the soft and gentle light of the sun peeked in through the transparent chambray curtains drawn over the two windows.

Returning to Rio, he went to find António Silva at the bar to ask him for advice on what direction his life should take. He had brought some money with him and he was thinking about buying a property in the country that would make him a profit. Silva was willing to lend him the money he needed. While they were talking with their elbows on the bar, a shadow appeared in the doorway that Silva recognised from his bearing and identified from his memory of him, even though he was not paying particular attention. It was Bajeca, who was from a village in the north of Madeira and was a chance visitor to the shops of people from the island. Despite the bad reputation that he had among his compatriots, they did not turn their backs on him. They called him a liar because he was never straight in business deals. They said there was a swindle wherever he pitched his tent. But even though they criticised him for being an adventurer, his compatriots still did business with him.

"What, Mr. Artur over here!"

"I came to try out Brazil. If it's good to me, I'll stay."

And with a hospitable air, Bajeca exclaimed, "Come to my place, Mr. Artur. Come and see how business is done."

"Is it far?"

"In Juiz de Fora. It takes a half day by train."

And they left with the sun heating the air and blazing down on the streets and the shiny green leaves of the exuberant vegetation in the gardens.

***

Artur liked the fields and the animals that Bajeca was looking after. He thought that maybe he could start his new life by trying farming and getting the maximum results out of it. His attention was caught by the orange grove and the wire fenced pasture for raising cattle.

"Do you want to sell this place?"

"I'll sell it."

"How much do you want for it?"

"Six hundred thousand cruzeiros."

"I'll give you five hundred thousand."

"It's a done deal."

The land measured sixty hectares. It had fifteen thousand orange trees and in the middle of these was a sugar cane plantation. In another part of the land was the fenced-in area with three Zebu bulls, a stable with four breeding cows and a calf, a shelter with seven pigs and two henhouses with three hundred hens. Included in the deal was a cart to take the produce to be swallowed up by the hungry mouths at the market.

After renting a small, two storey house on the edge of the farm, Artur started work with great hopes. He enlarged the henhouses and hired a black labourer to help him with the work. But, one morning,

when the black man was ploughing with the motorized plough, an Italian came to get it. He was a tall, skinny man.

"I bought everything that's here," said Artur.

"No, that plough belongs to me. I lent it to Bajeca about three months ago. But I can sell you it."

"How much do you want?"

"Four hundred cruzeiros, and that's cheap."

Artur's mind was too full of that scoundrel Bajeca to have any other solution, except to buy it. After digging drainage ditches, he planted a bed of vegetables that he knew would be much sought after in the market. On Maundy Thursday, he filled the cart as full as he could with cabbages, carrots, turnips and yams, as well as forty chickens and two pigs. The black horse, well hitched up, pulled the cart. Sitting on the seat, Artur held the reins while his labourer held onto the three big baskets covered with wire netting that served as a coop for the hens. The black man, whose eyes were more Oriental than African, would have been an exotic type of human being who confused anthropologists. His protruding jaw showed that there had been some strange kind of cross-breeding. He was of medium height, with an egg-shaped head, and looked somewhere between thirty and forty years old. A good tempered, obedient man, Leonel had taken a liking to his boss. As he knew the goods on the markets, he had become Artur's right hand man. As this was the first day of the market, the main street was full of carts. It was a warm, windless morning but it was drizzling and the people felt like staying under the awnings. They unloaded the cart right at the entrance to the market.

"How are you, Colonel?"

"Did you bring much to sell?"

"Just what you can see."

The local people filled the morning, bumping into each other as they searched for the bargains. The best produce ran out quickly. Artur was lucky in his first encounter with this multitude of people who clustered like bees round a honey pot. Everything was sold. When he got home, jubilant at the hundreds of cruzeiros that he had earned, he unharnessed the horse and sent Leonel off with it to feed it. When he had gone a few metres, Artur called out to him:

"Who was that colonel that was at the market?"

"You know, he's not an army colonel but a rich man. He's a father to the immigrants. He lends money."

"Does he live here?"

"Yes. He lives in the city but as he's one of the biggest farmers in Minas he spends weeks there on his land. He has his offices in the city."

"OK, OK!"

Leonel tied the horse up next to another older horse and fed it. After this, he continued through the orange grove, stopping to smell the most abundant of the little white stars. He felt a desire to see the little trees looking like Christmas trees, all loaded with big orange fruits.

This idea led to the thought that the harvest would make his boss rich. He had been well trained during his life as a semi-slave to the white man and never felt like rebelling against whoever fed him. It had been a long time since he had had a boss but the last but one he had worked for had been a Spaniard who returned to Seville after making a fortune on a beet plantation. For a number of years the Colonel had paid him for his services but when the farm machinery had been handed over to technicians and the oxen were sold off, he had been let go. He decided to go to the city, to Rio de Janeiro, and work for himself, trying out the vagabond-like life of a messenger boy.

A week after he had signed the deed for the land, Artur was wondering how to get a profit from it. It would be a good idea to get some cattle of good stock, and he had been told before he left Madeira that Brazil had some fine animals. He tried to find out in Rio. One morning when the sun was fierce, he was walking round the garden, looked up and saw the figure of a man standing in a doorway, with bitter melancholy showing on his dark face. As he had experience with the common people from his days spent with cattle dealers, grocers and the customers in the shoemaker's shop, the man inspired him with confidence. He went up to him and asked him if he wanted to be hired to work in the country. The reply was in the affirmative. They got off the afternoon train in Juiz de Fora and after greeting this and that neighbour on the way, they went into the house. Artur showed the black man the property and told him what he was to do.

"Don't worry, I won't be idle," he said in a friendly, submissive way.

And so he fixed and drove the cart and on his return tied up the horse and fed it. When he came out of the orange grove, he saw a short, fat man with a thick, greying moustache and piercing eyes leaning on the wall near the door. Leonel was about to go away when the man called to him.

"Are you from here?"

"Yes, sir."

"Isn't there a cart here?"

"There's ours, the boss's."

Go tell him I've come for it."

"Who loaned it to you?"

"It's mine! It's mine! It cost me money."

"You can't take anything away without the boss knowing."

"Ok."

"So, come with me."

And they turned to the right, round a fence and along a path to the road in front of Artur's poverty-stricken little house. Leonel beat on the door with the palm of his hand. The door opened.

"This gentleman has come for the cart."

"What cart?"

"Your cart."

As if he had just got out of bed, rudely awakened, Artur opened his eyes wide and stammered at the newcomer, "That cart is mine. I bought it."

"No! I lent it to Bajeca."

"Show me a paper written and signed by Bajeca."

The man reached his hand into his coat pocket and pulled out half a sheet of paper folded in two. He opened it and gave it to Artur.

After confirming that there had been a loan, red with anger, Artur shouted, Liar! Thief! He's going to pay!" And then, sadly, "And I left my home to be swindled by a bandit. Do you see the misfortune that befallen me?"

"But where is Mr. Bajeca?"

"Good question. After signing the deed to the property I haven't laid eyes on him. He was supposed to come here with me to give me some advice on the business but I haven't seen him again since he robbed me. Now he's going to run away from me, the scoundrel."

"Sir, Brazil is full of thieves."

"Ok. You can take the cart since it's yours but I'm going to take out the two planks that I used as seats."

And to Leonel:

"Go with the gentleman while I put my farm boots on."

Closing the door and taking off his slippers, Artur thought about the cart, which had been his right arm. Without it his business was finished. How could he sell the oranges and hens and pigs and all that the land was producing? If the man would sell him it, he wouldn't have to look for another one. And where was there one? It would take all the money he had earned in a few months. He cheered himself up by cursing Bajeca, who would pay for it all at once, some day.

He went out and turned round to lock the door. He adjusted his jacket, as the collar was turned up, put his hand in his inside pocket to make sure that he had his receipt book, and in ten minutes he met up with the newcomer, who thought that this was good farming land with excellent pasture for grazing cattle.

"Do you really need the cart?"

"I bought two horses and I have my chores to do. I know the market. My family and I live off the business."

"Do you know of anyone who would rent me a cart?"

"It's not easy. Anyone who has one won't want to be without it."

"You're from here; if you want, you can order a new cart from a workshop. You'd do me a great favour if you'd sell me yours."

So, the conversation went on and became cordial enough for the owner of the cart to come to an agreement with Artur, who bought the cart on very good terms.

CHAPTER XII

The years went by. Hot, rainy days and cooler, dry days. Week after week the business went well.

Artur was piling up the cruzeiros while his feverish imagination made plans to enlarge the farm, to increase the number and value of the things he grew and to enlarge the wire chicken coops for the third time. He bought a few more head of cattle and Leonel looked after them as if he were their owner. He petted them, the cow with the black spots, the one with the brown patches and all the rest, curving his hands to fit the flanks of the animals. And they waved their tails, enjoying the feel of his hands.

Artur thought hard about how he could make his fortune in a few years and then go home to Madeira. He wrote to his wife telling her about his success in business, Bajeca's trickery and the devotion of the black man, who was such a good friend that he might have known him since he was a boy.

All this while, dreaming at night and daydreaming by day, he made imaginary plans to buy another farm; one would be run by him and the other by Leonel, and he would hire the workers he needed by the week. One cart was already not enough to transport the cattle that he was slaughtering and butchering and the chickens and eggs and vegetables. The produce from his farm was famous. At the market, the best that was for sale came from Artur's farm.

One pale, calm afternoon, when he was counting the hens in the coops, it looked as though a bucket of water was about to be dumped out of the bellies of the pregnant clouds on the horizon. He hurried away in the direction of his house. As he coming through the gate, the owner of the next door farm came up to him and asked him if he was interested in buying his land. He said he intended to go to Ceará, where most of his wife's family was. He was asking 800,000 cruzeiros. With what he could get from the cattle, what he grew on the land and the cart, which was included in the deal, Artur could get back the 800,000 in two years. The deal was very tempting but he only had 400,000 cruzeiros. If he could only get a loan. Artur said that he would give the man his reply next day. Going into the house, he sat down on a stool and, with his elbows on his knees and his head in his hands, he began to think about the problem of raising the money to buy the farm next door. He thought of getting a loan from the bank for the 400,000 cruzeiros but he didn't know anyone who would put in a good word for him. And his friend Silva lived in Rio. Suddenly, an inspiration came to him from the recesses of his memory: Leonel could vouch for him and talk to the millionaire colonel. If he had a good year, maybe wealth would come knocking on his door.

Next morning, the cows were lowing as they waited to be fed. Leonel filled the manger with fresh grass, put on his white jacket and went to town.

It was the end of the week, Friday. This was the day that Colonel Justino only closed his office at eight o'clock at night. Fearing a refusal, since the Colonel was open enough to let the egotism of a miser show through, Leonel walked along the side of the building where the Colonel lived, as if he was afraid to be seen looking timid. The street door, which was painted a lustrous black, was open. He went up the steps. On the right, he could see inside through a half open door. Seated at a mahogany desk, the Colonel was arranging papers. When he heard someone come in, he raised his head.

"It's you, Leonel!"

They talked and when the matter had been explained to him, the Colonel agreed to make a loan to the Portuguese immigrant from Madeira.

Buying the farm next door to the one that had belonged to Bajeca made Artur prosper. Every week now, his two carts were the first to supply his customers at the market with fresh produce, which was always picked when ripe. And day labourers worked on the land.

One day, when returning from doing business, Artur noticed a chubby brunette with bewitching eyes the colour of almonds. And the she-devil bewitched him on the spot. They started to talk. By next day, she had become Artur's mistress and was moving in with him on the farm. Originally from Bahia, when she was sixteen she had married a shop assistant, a drunkard. She ran away from him, despising him and soon replacing him as she was born with her blood in constant heat. Leonel predicted that no good would come of his boss's love affair.

Fifteen days had gone by and Artur had, of course, forgotten about his wife and children, when he received a letter from Maria Clara that said,

"I don't want to leave my family and go to Brazil where I might not get on."

His wife's news had come at a good time. He never wrote to her again. The woman from Bahia made him give up his family, Maria Clara, the children and his home.

In truth, his love affair with the woman from Bahia was a spell, of sex. This alone was enough to give her control over him in all his business activities. With no will of his own, like an automaton, unaware, he did not shrink from her spendthrift caprices. Two summers in Copacabana did away with the profit from the farm that he had scrimped and saved in an unconquerable desire to do well, lighting up his soul with the distant light of the sun as it opened up a path through life in the day by day existence of the ever-expanding universe that would end in Juiz da Fora. But he could not see that the horizon was closing in on his sun, his hope and his struggle. The future that had propelled him like a rocket across the sea and the sky of the Brazil of his daydreams was full of troubled water that would suddenly be absorbed into the parched soil of the tropics.

He and the adventuress spent the best fruits of his labour. In the first few months of her married life with Artur, she began to show the inveterate habits of an ambitious girl whose days consisted of mornings spent lying in a luxurious bed or inventing an excess of luxury in the best room in the house, which had been extended to suite her taste, or enjoying the lazy afternoons lying in a hammock that Leonel had strung between two lemon trees that beautified the more spacious area where the cattle grazed.

She did not lack for expensive jewellery bought with Artur's hard-earned money.

Then she began to want to go to the cinema every week and to get to know cities that she had heard were very grand. And while she couldn't give herself airs by having a car, she was not satisfied with life. She was interested in the pleasures of spending money, wherever it came from, on constant trips and changing cars.

The business continued but the profit disappeared on extraordinary expenses.

One summer night, Leonel heard something odd on the farm, a confused noise, a trampling, that he could hardly hear in the heavy silence of the night.

He got up, put on his trousers and cotton jacket and peeked out. He could just hear the sound of the animals' hooves about a kilometre away in the chestnut grove. As a boy a belief in witchcraft would have penetrated deep in his soul, but this was real. The same thick silence that stuck to everything held him fast. He went back into his room but he could not sleep. As the sun rose, he went to the stable. He counted the cows and saw that the black cow and a calf had been stolen. He promised himself that he would catch the thieves and teach them a lesson that would mark them like a branding iron.

Meanwhile, in the monotonous passing of the days that end and those that enliven man's existence, Artur was astounded by the bitter fact that his profits were dwindling away.

After the two summers spent in Copacabana, his lover decided to enjoy two weeks in Caxambu because the waters there would be good for her health. Artur went home to Juiz de Fora.

It was in Caxambu that, at the end of the last week, she met up with a good looking man, who seemed to her to be handsome and have gentlemanly manners, and who was always alone and appeared to be preoccupied. She put aside any thoughts of Artur. So, he courted her, seeing in her the pretentious manners of a coquette and convinced that it would be an adventure that no one would talk about.

He put out the bait at tea time. As she was alone at a table, he went up and asked if she minded his company. The woman from Bahia smiled. And so the flirting began.

"Are you from far away?"

"I'm from Bahia."

"There are such flowers in your part of the country!"

"Don't be silly!"

And the conversation went on so long that indiscreet glances could be seen looking at the couple in the corner.

Next day, the two of them went by car out beyond the suburbs of Caxambu.

***

In spite of the progress made by the farm in raising cattle and growing a variety of crops, the bank cut off Artur's credit. That woman was costing a lot of money: buying a car, renting a flat in Copacabana, the orders for fashionable items that constantly caught her eye and her imagination, the trips, the hotels, all weighed heavily on his debilitated savings, all because of his lover. And, to add to this, more and more animals were being stolen in the dead of night. After the two cows, a horse disappeared and the thieves tried to take away a cart. The reports to the police dragged on. Their investigations did not turn up any clues that would lead them to the robbers.

Leonel knew many people in the area but he did not know how dishonest some of the merchants were. From the sale of three beasts for slaughter to a certain Celestino, Artur was owed about one thousand cruzeiros that he was never paid. But this did not happen because he was an immigrant; not keeping one's word was common in those parts. In despair, Leonel went every week on horseback several kilometres to find the door of Celestino's house locked. And however much he knocked, no one came to the window and there was no sound of footsteps. Mortified, he went home unwilling to face Artur as he knew how things were going. Every day he gave him advice, trying to make him see that the woman from Bahia would only leave him in peace when she had taken the rest of his belongings.

"That woman is your downfall. All she does is spend and she must be sleeping with other men."

"When I know that she's been cheating on me, that will be the end."

Artur was in this worried frame of mind when a certain Alberto Aloísio from Boaventura, who was now living in São Paulo, came to the house. He said that he had come to see him. He knew that his friend was almost the "owner" of Juiz de Fora. Intrigued by Aloísio's visit, Artur asked how he had found out. And Aloísio, a talking machine, convinced him of the old truth: the earth may be big but it's small for people from the same place. They were attracted to each other; there was always someone who knew this or that person and where he was. That was why he was there. After three days at the home of his fellow countryman, where he ate and slept, he gave him the news that he was going back to Madeira by boat, taking back more than 40,000 escudos worth of used tyres. He was going to try that business. And next morning Artur went to the docks to say goodbye to Aloísio.

This unexpected meeting with a compatriot left Artur thoughtful and abstracted. Why did people emigrate? Aloísio went to São Paulo, had some bad jobs, had bad luck , years without seeing his family and he was going back home with 40,000 escudos worth of used tyres. The hope of making one's fortune was like the summer sun. Looking at himself, he trembled when he thought of ending up like Aloísio. Those who emigrate should only take care of business. That was how he started. But man is weak. Why hadn't his wife come to live with him?

CHAPTER XIII

At that time, the Ribeiro brothers from Faial came to live near Juiz de Fora in the hopes of making their fortune. They left the Island for Rio de Janeiro on the day before Easter. They brought Artur a letter asking him to help them. It came from a cattle dealer in Santana with whom he had done business. And as country people want to be in the country, they could not change their surroundings for any physical or human environment very different from the social circle in which they had been born and lived or from that way of life. José Ribeiro, who was forty years old and thin with a pale face and blue eyes, desperately wanted to succeed. His brother Luís, who was five years younger, had also inherited a fighting spirit from his ancestors. They promised each other that they had to find a profitable business so that, if luck was with them, they could go back to their wives and live out their dreams.

They missed their homeland, their people and their language. But their hostility waned as they became familiar with the place and travelled to the nearby villages. They had the art of attracting people because of their good manners, offering a drink of Madeira rum to the people they knew. Artur told them at their first meeting how to make their fortune.

He sent Leonel to find out specific information about the farms that were for sale. He looked very hard and found a large, partially abandoned farm about four kilometres from the railway that had fruit trees, pasture, skinny cattle and a ruined house with a lot of its tiles missing.

José Ribeiro, the more practised in the art of contracts, found the owner, who was living in the city and had a sausage shop. He had not been able to stand life in the provinces after he became a widower. He greeted the Portuguese man pleasantly and sang the praises of the farm, making it sound easy to bring it back into production. It was a very healthy place and the people were very friendly, he said.

The Ribeiro brothers bought the farm. They rebuilt the house, worked the land and started a cattle business just like the one that they had been born into back in Faial. And after buying a pickup truck to carry heavy loads and take long journeys, they settled down in Juiz de Fora, blessing the day that they had arrived in Brazil. But they were not free from problems or from evil doers from outside the region. One night, when they were in the bedroom, they heard footsteps outside the house and then horses whinnying in the stable. Luís, who was the braver one, took the hunting rifle from beside the bed, put on his coat, went down the stairs and quietly opened the door. Two shadows that might be hiding another one were standing in front of the stable. He fired a shot, disturbing the stillness of the air and the silence of the night. Whoever it was picked up his heels and ran away. And they continued to live in peace and to work hard, with a daily routine in which the sweat of their brow was repaid by their progress in life. In an immigrant's heart, the idea of going home is as indelible as the memory of the land where he was born.

Meanwhile, the woman from Bahia, with her over-vigorous female nature that was always in rut, was in Caxambu having an adventure with the holidaymaker. In order to make herself more seductive, when she sat next to him she crossed her legs so that the men could not take their eyes off her, showing off her unmarried voluptuousness and the warmth of her light skin. It was the weekend, but the enchantment of her idyll made her prolong her stay. She phoned Artur to tell him to come and pick her up in a week's time because the rest, she hinted, did her nerves more good than a whole season on the farm. He agreed reluctantly with her wish although the cruzeiros were getting fewer and he had failed in his most hopeful plans by selling a large part of the herd of cattle.

Leonel tried to restore some stability to the financial situation with pigs, but the expenses were greater than the income, due to the caprices of the woman from Bahia. In addition, there was greater competition, more produce coming from the land and animals for sale at higher prices, and Artur was not cooperating as he had when his thoughts and his actions were free. That she-devil was the curse of his life.

He built a large tin roof and surrounded it with wooden walls to make the animals safer from any possible attacks, just like one built by the Ribeiro brothers.

Later in the year, Maria Clara wrote him a letter full of complaints, in which she accused her husband of being a bad father who had stopped taking any notice of his children. It didn't matter about her. She despised him. Artur tore up the letter and delightedly looked at the portrait of the woman from Bahia in its gold frame standing on the dressing table. Immediately, he sat down on the edge of the bed and thoughtfully remembering the recent past, he became aware of a certain feeling of indignation because the woman he had tied himself to had to be flighty, just as Leonel had said. But then the heavy, sad thought lightened as he thought of the curvaceous, untiring body of the woman who held him in thrall.

"Boss!"

"What is it?"

"It's Mr. Ribeiro."

The car stopped, silently, at the entrance to the farm. Artur looked out of the window and felt very small compared to Ribeiro, who in less than a year had already become well known in the area as a wealthy Portuguese entrepreneur. And the thought of that woman made him feel worse, because she was the cause of his delirium, his discredit in the local economy. Wilfully clearing his mind so that he could show his guest a good face, he went up to Ribeiro looking jubilant.

"How's business?"

"Couldn't be worse, Artur!"

And José Ribeiro told him at length about the expense of rebuilding the demolished warehouses, the walls on the farm, buying tools and above all the difficulty of finding good cattle.

He praised his good neighbours, a couple from Minho, and the loan that this couple had helped him get from the bank. He hoped that in a few years' time he and his brother could go home and never think of emigrating again. It wasn't that living there was bad, as they had good health and had made money. It was just that he wasn't in his own home in the village where his wife and children were. When night fell, he heard the birds singing so loudly it was frightening. And he liked to see the sea because he'd been born near it. He and his brother had thought more than once about sending for their families, but what for? They were convinced that if they were all there living together with everything they needed, would it be like having Faial there with them and them living on their own land? That wasn't the whole truth: it wasn't really like that. The words that they spoke were not what they felt. If they had been born there in Juiz de Fora, they would have been at home. But that didn't happen. They were foreigners and would be until they died if they continued to live there. There was no land in the world that you could buy that was like the one where you were born. Artur agreed with Ribeiro's ideas but inside him, he wished they would stop talking to him about Madeira so that he could forget about his family.

***

On Thursday morning, Artur left suddenly for Caxambu. His lover was not aware of his decision as she had put off her return for a week. He was going early to cut down the expenses. When he arrived at the hotel he asked the receptionist for the key to the room.

"Madam took it with her."

"A long time ago?"

"She left with another guest."

Artur felt the kind of jealousy that leads to crime. He knew that he was being betrayed. He had no doubt of it. She was cheating on him. Just more proof that Leonel was right in advising him to leave her, because the business was sliding into irretrievable losses.

After a few moments of wild imaginings and contradictory thoughts, he calmed down. He walked away, wandering about the more secluded spots, looking around without seeing anything, wanting to react to his depression but feeling defeated. Then, suddenly, as if he had acquired new heart, he walked away quickly, straight to the street by the railway line. His head down, not seeing the trees on either side, he wondered if he should go back to Juiz de Fora, consigning the woman from Bahia to the depths of hell, or should he surprise her, confirm her infidelity and slap her? That was what he should do, so that no doubts remained in his mind. And so he turned back. He thought again and decided that if he did catch her, it was not a good idea to create a scandal. She was not worth it. So, thinking, with his eyes on the ground and not looking into the distance, he found himself back in front of the hotel. He was going to go in but instead, acting on an impulse, he went to stand under a palm tree. As the bright sunlight was hurting his eyes, he squatted down behind the tree. At that moment, a car stopped in front of the hotel doorway. He recognized the car. She got out of the driver's side. Then an individual in a cream coloured suit got out and put his arm around her waist. She lifted her head and their lips met. It was just as the bodies came together when Artur, like an animal finding its prey, rushed up to the woman from Bahia and, to the amazement of her companion, said in scornful tones,

"You whore!"

The scene occurred with no spectators, with no drama, in the calm of a lazy afternoon. And while the other two took refuge in the hotel, Artur took possession of the Willys that had cost him several thousand cruzeiros and drove off swiftly to Juiz de Fora.

Now there was a problem to solve, a delicate situation: to put his business back on track after his lover had demolished it. The farm he had bought from Bajeca was mortgaged. The small cart needed to be repaired or replaced. Only one cart was carrying the goods, the one from the big farm.

Week by week the cattle were disappearing and he could not replace them because his lack of capital made it impossible to take on any debts. Artur's adventure had closed all the doors to credit to him.

And the problems continued. A sickness killed hundreds of chickens and a contagious fever did away with the best pigs. And worse still, sometime one evening before filling a cartload of oranges and birds, Leonel woke up in confusion as he heard an uproar that seemed to come from the herd of zebu cattle. The noise was confusing. He opened the window and, listening carefully, he realized that the thieves were up to their tricks. The coal black night made it easy to take the cattle and run away. He got dressed and woke his boss. Loading his hunting rifle, Artur went out to Leonel who took the bulls-eye lantern to light the twisting path through the dry scrub. When they came to the fence, a gunshot rang out. Two shadows ran off into the darkness.

Suddenly, there was an anguished cry, "Ay, I've been killed!"

Leonel fell face down onto a pile of sugarcane straw. In the confusion, Artur fired at the shadow in the distance and grabbed hold of Leonel, whose side was bleeding. He had been knifed and the wound looked deep. With difficulty, Artur hoisted the black man into the car and drove at top speed to the hospital. However, having lost too much blood, Leonel did not survive the emergency operation.

The slow investigations by the police were useless; they did not find the murderer. There were prisonsful of felons on the run. All was in vain. Artur's sorrow at the loss of his old friend put an end to any hope of his remaking his life as a merchant.

The other man had had a rare brotherly affection for Artur both in the prosperous days of good profits and during the financial disaster caused by the woman from Bahia. Artur missed his advice urging him to work, his sensible opinions, his spirit of sacrifice, the way he encouraged him in the fight to succeed. The farm lay abandoned.

He continued to work at the business for two months, loading the cart himself, taking care of the animals and cutting up the cattle into quarters for the butcher, but the cruzeiros that he saved were not enough to pay the loan payments that were due each month. Despairing of managing things and making his fortune in Juiz de Fora, one night he began to take stock of the few resources that remained after paying his debts. Heartsick, he realized that after selling the land that was not mortgaged he would only have the money he needed to emigrate again, for he was leaving Brazil to try his luck in Venezuela. He had acquaintances there and even friends. One of these friends, with whom he exchanged letters from time to time, António Martins, had told him in one of his letters, as he still remembered, to go to Venezuela and set up as a shoemaker. This craft had a future for anyone who, like him, was a master craftsman. It would be wrong, probably, not to take advantage of this advice at a time when enthusiasm has the eyes of a lynx and the wings of an eagle. He was still young enough. At fifty years of age, and with his experience in Juiz de Fora, by sixty he could be someone back home and buy some land that would make a profit. He stayed awake almost all night. And as if inspired to resolve the matter, he decided to liquidate what he had in the best way possible, by going to the Ribeiro brothers. So, in the morning, after swallowing a cup of coffee, he got into the car and set off for the Ribeiro brothers' farm. When he got onto the open road, he accelerated, anxious to cross the plain that stretched back like a desert behind him, with a few houses here and there by the side of the road. His eyes were turned inward, reliving his life in Achada, the Achada of his childhood. The disappointments he had suffered there brought back the opposite memories, of the happy times he had spent, and he was nostalgic for the local festivals and the bustle of the harvest.

The first buildings came into view and there were people on both sides of the road. After a few minutes, Artur received a hospitable welcome at the Ribeiro brothers' farm. He felt shy, uncomfortable and very small at the sight of the enormous estate where a crew of men was working the land. There seemed to be no end to the avenue that left to the big yellow painted house.

"Look, Mr. Artur. All this is our work. We want to get the most out of it when we sell up."

Artur tried hard not to show what he was feeling on his face. He put on a broad smile as in agreement.

He was amazed to see a new van and a new lorry, and a barn filled with all the tools needed to work the land. The sugar cane waved in the fragrant breeze.

And he thought to himself, "If I didn't have such a bad head on me, I would have had luck too!"

"Now, Mr. Artur, we're going to show you a surprise. Come this way. Look inside the greenhouse!"

"What's that?"

"It's a vine shoot from Faial. We didn't rest till they sent us one. That's our homeland living over here. Let's see if it roots and produces grapes."

After making a meticulous visit to all the corners of the property to see that the work had been carried out according to José

Ribeiro's plans, the conversation turned to praise for the Portuguese emigrants who were taming the land that was hardest to work.

With some timidity, afraid of a refusal, Artur explained his situation and his wish to immigrate to Venezuela in order to continue being a shoemaker. He didn't even mind being hurt financially. He needed to leave Brazil.

"We know your land and although we are not very much interested, we'll buy everything and pay off your debts. Tomorrow let's go to the city and do the deal. Ten o'clock outside the notary's office."

CHAPTER XIV

That hot, misty afternoon, when he left Juiz de Fora on board the train that took him to Rio de Janeiro, Artur had some unforgettable memories on his mind, however much he wanted to forget them. One, painful and sad, was etched on his heart and on his retina from his early days as an immigrant. It was the humble, submissive face of the unfortunate man who had been his friend, as close to him as his shadow while he was alive. Another, equally painful but negative, hurt his manly pride. He wanted to eradicate that memory like one kills a venomous snake, the image of the woman from Bahia.

When he arrived in Rio, the flood of emotions stopped. He picked up his suitcase and went to a travel agency where he bought a ticket for the night plane. Then he went to the airport, putting the ticket in his wallet with his passport.

The plane flight did not frighten him. In Caracas, a taxi took him to António Martins' house on the edge of the city. He searched for a neighbourhood where he could best ply his trade. He rented a shop on Real Salana Grande Street and set up as a shoemaker. He bought some modern lasts and the best quality hides. And he began to make handmade shoes that awakened the interest of the lower class Spaniards and Madeirans scattered around the outlying suburbs. The work was cleaner than dealing in cattle. He had fewer worries since he could not make big money all at once. Even so, little by little, the bolivars began to pile up.

And he planned his future, once again showing the versatility and lack of persistence that characterised all his engrossing start ups.

He rented a room from António Martins until he could afford his own place. Getting used again to the life he had always had, the frenzy of adapting to and learning a new trade lessened. He got up early and, after walking for a quarter of an hour, he reached the shop and set to work. Sometimes he mended shoes, or he put on heels, or he sewed calfskin uppers for men's shoes. He was never idle; he always had something to do. At night he went to his room to sleep and get up early the next day. At the end of the second month, when he did his accounts, he used almost all the bolivars that he had saved up to buy a suit and the rest he spent on some tinned food to have for lunch at the shop. He needed to save. This was what many of his fellow countrymen did and that was why they had money in the bank. In a foreign land, they all suffered bad times and even took on jobs that they had not had where they were raised, either in a village or in the city. A month after settling in Venezuela, one morning, he recognized a compatriot who was supposed to be rich pushing a cart, selling almonds. He looked at him carefully and he was not wrong. He thought that in that country the struggle to live was harder than it had been in the interior of Brazil where you could get what you needed to feed you out of the ground. At night, after closing the shop, his dinner consisted of two eggs and half a cup of coffee at the Martins' house.

He began to get to know some of his customers who were from mainland Portugal, from Beira Alta. They were good, honest people. The son of the owner of a bakery made him an offer that he accepted: he sold him the business and gave him the shop with all the shoemaking tools. It was a good deal. But now he had to find a new trade as the bolivars were running out because he was not working. He couldn't live on air or abuse the generosity of António Martins, to whom he paid a ridiculously small sum as rent for his room. It was in his nature to want change and new emotions, to put himself into distressing situations and then take on untried jobs in order to make the fortune that he coveted and constructed in his immigrant's soul. Now, in Venezuela, he recognized his lack of persistence in any way of life that he took on.

At a beer bar where the Portuguese met, he got to know a man from the Alentejo, a thin, middle-aged man with a moustache with whom he had pleasant conversations. They talked about business. Artur confided in him that he was looking around for somewhere to set up in his profession.

And they exchanged impressions:

"I have a shoe shop with a good clientele. But for some months now I've been thinking of selling it and taking up some other kind of work," said the man.

"I did have one, as I told you, but it seems to me I should go back to my trade. If we can come to an agreement, I'll buy your shop. As it is, I've already lost my hopes of becoming a millionaire!"

And after drinking a few more glasses of beer, they agreed to sign the document next day in front of the notary.

Pleased with his purchase, Artur went back to his old trade on Organeta Avenue. However, the shop only sold factory-made shoes. As for shoemaking, the only repairs were putting studs on heels. That way of working was more profitable and less work; the bolivars dropped into the drawer more often. And he continued to save and to put money in the bank. For five months he lived for the shoe shop. His days were spent taking care of the shop, arranging the shoes on the shelves, dusting the glass counter. But he soon became bored. He got tired. He lost his patience with the customers who tried on lots of pairs of shoes, promised to come back next morning and never returned.

One day, when serving a young woman, a man in a tie came in with a briefcase in his hand. He looked at Artur oddly and said,

"Don't you remember me?"

"I've no idea," replied Artur.

"I'm Álvaro, of the Vilões family."

"From where?"

"From Canhas. Don't you remember the ox that my brother sold you? You even said that you'd never seen an animal with such a body, after all your years in the cattle business."

"Ah! Now I know. I remember that you were doing your papers to come over here."

"That's right. Nine years ago."

"When are you going back home?"

"Maybe next month. I just want to get rid of a little butchery because I don't want to work any more far from the family."

"Well, I was in Brazil and it's a year since I came here. I haven't had any luck but I wouldn't want to go back to Madeira with taking enough money to buy some land and build a house."

"Why don't you take the butcher's shop? There's no credit given there and the money comes in by the hour."

Artur was enthusiastic and replied, "I'll think about it. I'm interested in changing my way of life. In selling the shoe shop. I'm sick of putting up with some of the customers. You have to have a lot of patience and I'm losing it."

Álvaro said goodbye and set a time to meet again. Meanwhile, Artur started thinking about how to get rid of the shoe shop. This was only possible by transferring the lease. When he was closing the shop, suddenly, as if by magic, a possible idea came to him. His leathery face lit up and he felt the same excitement as if he were still young. Once again, he felt the will to succeed by fighting his weakness, a desire to persevere, without going broke, to go to the limit as if he was taking a long trip that would end at its destination. To be the owner of a butcher's shop there in a neighbourhood in Caracas! He was ready for a "meaty" business! Then the idea came, a sudden light showing him a path opening up in his night of despair; selling the shoe shop was at once a certainty about which he had no doubts. Just last week Bacalhau from Falca had come looking for him and had insisted that he sell him the lease on the shoe shop. He remembered the words that he had spoken at the shop counter:

"Mr. Artur, these are 85,000 escudos in Portuguese money. You can't lose, dealing with me."

"It's a round figure: 90,000."

Bacalhau gave a pale smile.

The scene had taken place just a few days ago. Artur decided to go to Bacalhau's house. And, as he lived in the same neighbourhood as Martins, before going home to bed, he went down a dark alley and found Bacalhau playing cards with a cousin who had just come from Curaçao.

"Good evening."

"I was just telling my cousin about you," said Bacalhau.

"Good things or bad things?"

"When the Portuguese live abroad, they never say bad things about their own kind. We always want good to come to everyone. But, as I was saying, I was talking to my cousin about you a while ago, Mr. Artur, because of the shoe shop."

"I'm ready to sell it."

"Wait a minute, Mr. Artur. We'll finish the game."

He put his cards down on the table.

"I win, cousin! One hand left to go."

Bacalhau shuffled the cards and dealt each of them six cards.

Artur, who was watching the game, was there in body but not in spirit. His mind was far away, in Achada. He remembered going to the neighbours' houses and playing three-handed whist on long December nights, joking with his friends.

"The game's over," said Bacalhau. "So, Mr. Artur, are you going to get rid of the shop or not?"

"The deal is on the table!"

"I haven't told you yet why I'm buying the shoe shop. But as I'm not making a secret of it, I can tell you that the shop is for my brother, who should be arriving from Madeira in a week's time. That's why I'm interested. I won't argue about five thousand more or five thousand less. I'll pay you the ninety thousand."

Having pocketed the money for his shop, Artur went to see Álvaro and they came to an agreement: from a shoe shop to a butcher's shop.

The butcher's was in a good location on Victoria Avenue. The neighbourhood abounded in customers and Artur did not have any time on his hands. When he added up the takings in the evening and saw the business he had done, he realised that he had never had such a profitable business.

Because the bolivars were piling up and his bank account was growing, his ambition was increasing at the same pace as the money that came in so easily each day. He moved from his little hutch at Martins' house to a comfortable room in the house of a Portuguese couple, nearer the shop. His vivid imagination never turned from doing something concrete: another business that would contribute to increasing his bank account. He heard about an eighty hectare farm and bought it. He spent nearly one hundred and fifty thousand bolivars on necessary improvements, restoring the barns, building a wall around the property and building pens for the cattle. But he had to divide his time between the butcher's shop and the farm. He hired an employee to replace him at the butcher's while he went to the farm. But when night came he was exhausted and felt sorry that he had diversified his activities. Then came the disappointment. He sold a number of cows to a Gonçalves from Calheta for one hundred thousand bolivars. It would have been a good deal if Gonçalves had kept his word. Artur trusted his friend but he was cheated. The man never came back. He went off into the interior without saying a word about his whereabouts to his house mate, who was from Paul. Artur learned his lesson. He was doing fine, earning more than most of his compatriots so why could he not rein in this eternal dissatisfaction? He had to stop being so ambitious. To do this, he thought about selling the farm. He advertised it and received two offers. He took the one that hurt less and lost ten thousand on the deal. After this, he went to sleep thinking about the butcher's shop and got up with the thought of it dancing before his eyes.

Starting in the first week in March, Artur noticed that a thin Spanish woman over the age of fifty, who stooped slightly but had flashing eyes that penetrated into the depths of his being, kept leaning on the counter and staying to chat. Each day the Spanish woman became more and more familiar and revealed more of her biography as a spinster.

"Why didn't you marry?"

She smiled, but it was a pale smile. She shrugged her shoulders and, because the shop was about to close, went away still smiling.

On his way home, Artur remembered the woman from Bahia, not trying to see her in his memory but rather repressing a spontaneous mental picture of her. The ugly spinster, whose eyes still sparkled with a youthful light, was in complete contrast to the other one, who had treated him so shamefully.

As the memory of that *femme fatale* faded, another image came into his mind, dimmed by the passage of time: that of Maria Clara, the mother of the children whom he would not recognise if he should happen to meet them. He had never had any photos but the image of Achada never left the back of his mind because he was born in that mountainous landscape.

The days went by. His friendship with the Spanish woman became so strong that one Sunday he went to her house. She lived in a three room apartment. She showed him the clean kitchen where the pans shone and the enamel stove had not a scratch on it. Afterwards, he saw the little sitting room where there was a table that shone like a mirror and two armchairs covered in good cloth. Finally, she led him into the bedroom. The bed, with its wine coloured bedspread and two lace trimmed pillows, stood on a chestnut coloured carpet.

Artur asked her why there were two pillows if she lived alone. With her eyes lit up with passion and with an obvious shyness in her words, she said, "For my beloved!"

"Where is he?"

"Here…"

"Me?"

"Yes!" And she threw her arms around his neck and kissed him on the mouth.

After that day, the spare pillow, which had been unused, stopped being a simple adornment. The Spanish woman's house became Artur's home. He was short of nothing: lunch and dinner on time and his clothes taken care of. In the first few years, the butcher's shop prospered but then other butcher's shops opened in the neighbourhood and the competition lessened his advantage. Profits fell. A legal dispute with the owner of the building cost him thousands of bolivars. Definitely life went on. But as time ages everything, it made the Spanish woman turn sixty and become uglier than ever. Her face became like parchment, with deep wrinkles and a moustache that gave her an androgynous appearance.

In spite of the comforts that he enjoyed, he began to hate himself because the woman no longer interested him as a woman. He stopped going home early and when he opened the door late at night and went into the room, the *señorita,* who had been waiting up for him, burst into tears, lamenting her wretched misfortune. He put on his pyjamas, lay down and did not say a word to explain why he was so late. He slept on the edge of the mattress, so as not to touch his companion. The relationship, which had never awakened in Artur the sincere affection that she had spontaneously and unselfishly given to him, came apart as easily as a badly tied knot in a piece of string.

CHAPTER XV

Inês's visit to Matilde's house was like consulting an oracle and receiving a decisive, heartening answer. The impressions that she had received from Matilde about her husband's income and the money that he sent home each month were all a happy prediction come true. She told Francisco all the details that her imagination had enlarged and transformed so as to bring about what she wanted, about how the happiness of her friend was in Antigua. She had taken a decision that had to be settled as soon as possible. To go to Venezuela.

"So, what do you think, Inês?"

"Look, borrow the money you need to pay for your ticket."

"I'm to go alone?"

"Yes. When you've earned enough for me and the children to go, I'll follow you. We're not selling anything. It's the shop that's caused the problem, because of the credit. What the land gives is enough to live on. And the cow is still giving milk to sell to the dairy."

"And who am I going to ask for the money? Nobody here in this parish! Everyone would get to know and they wouldn't help us, out of jealousy."

"I've got an idea. What if I ask Matilde?"

"Maybe that's a good idea."

The shop continued to bring in almost nothing. As Carolina was the eldest and most sensible of the children, she was already serving the customers when her father and mother were not there. A day rarely came when someone did not ask for credit.

"Please put it on the bill," said the stunted little barefoot boy.

And then the woman in the shawl, "Give me a litre of paraffin."

"We're waiting for the steamer to bring some."

This way of life had to end. Inês, who had very determined ideas, considered selling the lease on the shop. Before going to see Cambado, who had talked to Francisco one Sunday and in half words had suggested buying the business, she wrote to Matilde asking her to loan them the rest of the money so her husband could leave. The reply was not long in coming. The letter ended like this:

"Tell me how much you want. I'll lend you what you need. Matilde."

Cambado lived in Pastel. Although he was quite old, he did not want to have his son or his unmarried daughter to run the shop. He was born to be a shopkeeper and round about there, when his name was mentioned, someone always said, "He knows how to look out for himself."

That evening, after the day's business was over and he had closed the shop, Francisco waited for Cambado to be at home. Soon after, he knocked on the kitchen window where the light of the oil lamp could be seen through a crack

"Who is it?"

"Francisco from Achada."

Cambado came to the door. They talked over transferring the lease and the shop was sold.

On Monday morning, Inês and her husband went down to the city along the Torrinhas path. In Funchal, they went from office to office, helped by Matilde who had acquaintances at the government offices and the Martins agency.

Francisco booked a passage to Venezuela on board the *Cape Horn* for the end of December.

***

So, Francisco left from the city quay under a sky heavy with coal black clouds. He and Inês had said good bye in Achada.

The sea was calm for the first three days. In the smoking room, people played cards. The Spaniards played the accordion and gossiped, but Francisco felt sad as he was alone, could speak only his own language and had no wish to listen to the music reverberating round the saloon. He had no patience for watching the dancing. He went to his cabin early. The days that followed were very difficult for him as the sea was rough. He hardly ate. The boiled meat and the pasta made him feel queasy. Lying on his bunk, the painful memories of his wife and children made him wish that he had not left them to follow a dream in search of riches. However, his despair gave way to hope, to steadfastness, the courage to succeed in whatever the future might bring.

He did not know why the Venezuelan authorities came aboard to receive the immigrants whose names were on a list. His was at the bottom. They took them to a hotel and lodged them there for twenty-five days, during which time those who did not know anyone from home in the city wandered around looking for employment. As he had the address of a couple from Santana, Francisco stayed at their house.

He had very little money left to change into bolivars. One morning, as he was going to the bank, someone slapped him on the back. It was a well dressed man who asked him if he wanted to work in a factory. He felt his heart beat with a strange happiness, as if he had just received the news of having had some really good luck.

His life began to make sense, a purpose that depended on the strength of his arms: to provide for the welfare of his family and prepare his children for the future by giving them the education that he had never had.

At the factory, two hundred and eighty workers operated the machines and carried out the chemical dying process. The warehouses were filled with bolts of cloth. Other men loaded the lorries with thousands of packages.

The owner was a Jew, a man aged under fifty, of medium height and burly, without being fat. Not all the workers liked him, certainly, but Francisco could hardly say anything bad of him as he was generous, understanding and a friend to the Portuguese man. He let Francisco sleep in the factory so he did not have to spend money on travelling from the neighbourhood where he was living. Jokingly, he often said to him, "You're a citizen!" The factory was Francisco's home for nearly two years. He made some money that he put in the bank and with those bolivars he bought a bakery on Casa Nova Avenue. When he went to the owner's office at the end of the year to tell him that he was leaving because he had decided to send for his family and take over a business, the Jew was sad, but promised to help him if he needed it.

He rented a long one storey house with a tiled roof. He wrote Inês a very different letter from the previous ones, which filled her with immeasurable pleasure at the surprise. She was to book their tickets and come over on the first boat that stopped in Venezuela. Mad with happiness, she left her parents to take care of the fields and the cow. And because Francisco had sent her enough money for all the expenses, she packed the children's clothes and hers in a bag and took the bus to the city. Her daughter's godmother, Matilde, was waiting for them and she took care of the passports and the tickets. In two days' time the *Cape Horn* would be in port.

Matilde shared Inês's joy, enjoying the happiness in her simple soul, the way her hopes were being fulfilled, the plans for a reality that for years had been only an abstraction, an imaginary chimera that had been born, who knows how, up in the mountains of Achada do Castanheiro.

Five months had gone by since Francisco had arrived in Caracas and Matilde had already been paid the two thousand seven hundred escudos that she had lent them, a loan that had not been documented. After lunch on the day before they left, Inês asked Matilde to go with them to have their photo taken to take with them as a souvenir. They went to the Vicente photography studio.

Inês from Achada liked the backdrop with the sea view because she said that it would only be possible for her to find happiness by crossing the sea. From there, they went down João Tavira Street, turned into Aljube Street and went into Comachos, where Inês bought a trunk to put the clothes in, which she had brought down in bags.

***

When they went to the quay, a tearful Carolina kissed her godmother and hugged her in an embrace that seemed unending. Inês, meanwhile, was thinking about how much she owed Matilde, who had proved to be so sincere and whose sisterly gestures had engraved an eternal mark of gratitude on her soul, and she too wept with deep and painful nostalgia at the thought of leaving behind someone who had left such an impression on her. From the quayside, Matilde's waving handkerchief spoke as if it was stammering out the words that marked a moment that was never to be repeated: have a safe journey!

CHAPTER XVI

It was Sunday. Jorge Ratazana, or Tracis, the nickname that had been given to him, had changed. He had become responsible and was no longer insolent and wayward like his father, as he had been when he was a boy. He had picked up good manners since he had been going around in the company of Agostinho da Silveira, with whom he studied the theory of solfeggio to sing in church. On holy days and Sundays, after choir practice, they played whist for hours on end, while on Thursdays and Saturdays he was learning to play the mandolin with Teacher Jorge who was trying to organize a string musical group. He was also in the second year of high school. The previous Thursday, after the exercises of simple stretches of melody, the talk had turned to emigrating.

When I'm old enough, I'm going to Venezuela. Here in the village people just don't get on. They never stop wearing cream leather work boots," said José das Pingas' son.

"Do you think that everyone who goes away gets rich?" retorted Leonel.

"With good health and hard work, you can get what you want."

"When you don't spend everything you earn," said Teacher Jorge.

"I know it's necessary to be sensible," said Emilio Pingas. And going on with his reasoning, "If you don't have good health, hard work and good sense, you can get to have a hotel like the Pestana brothers in Ribeira Brava, that great big city hotel that cost millions. If you stay in Boaventura or any other village in Madeira, you can do alright but you'll never be rich. I'm willing to work so I can become rich. And I also say that if that happens, I have to help the poor people back home."

"By the way, Leonel, has your uncle Artur written?"

"My aunt hasn't heard from him for years."

"But they say he's a millionaire! He must live with some other woman over there to have forgotten what he left behind here."

And Professor Jorge picked up the mandolin that was lying on the table and began to tune it, holding his head in a way that showed up his lantern jaw.

"Everyone in place," he said. "Come on, Leonel! We're going to play that march you know."

"Teacher, the thickest string is messed up."

"Wait. Aníbal, give me that violin. Put the mandolins on the table."

And in the twinkling of an eye, all the instruments had been tuned and the trilling of the mandolins joined with the sound of the violin and filled the school room.

"Another week more and we can put on a show at the community centre. And before the show we'll ask Mr. Vegario and the lady teachers and the director to come and listen to the rehearsal."

It had been about twenty years since Jorge, the teacher, had come over the Torrinhas mountains to settle in Igreja. He was still very young then and got used to the rustic surroundings, which were primitive and hostile to any civilizing or educational pressure to create new habits of intelligence and the preliminaries to culture. Because he had a teacher's soul, he managed to inculcate a taste for the arts in the generations of boys and girls who had left the school in the recent past. He was proud, but not vainly, of his success, as he had taken his idea and associated it with a will to succeed. He created an acting group, despite the harsh and almost insurmountable opposition of the girls' parents. One of them, who lived in Falca, was a natural actress. As her mother could not always come with her, when she did not come there was no rehearsal.

Jorge adapted a story by Trindade Coelho, *My Loves*[9], as a play. Narcisa from Falca, who was fifteen years old, seemed to live the role that she was playing, so natural were her words and her gestures. She was tall and slim, with a dark skin, jet black eyes and hair that was also jet black, and she was a pensive girl who was

---

[9] "Os Meu Amores" in the original

often absent minded. Her abstraction was, however, balanced by the liveliness of a swallow.

Because of this, she stood out from the other girls, attracting attention to herself, and by herself she could dominate a crowd of spectators.

The renaissance that Jorge, the teacher, brought to the human material that he had found stagnating, to the potential that he found amidst the lack of stimuli, reverberated around the villages and hamlets of the north of the island. When a concert or a show was announced at the community centre, the room became too small and people came from far and wide, from the depths of the north-west, burning to see Narcisa act.

But because human beings cannot prevent things moving from beginning to end, and change is inherent to life, a lad from Falca, who was living in Africa, came back to visit his family. One December night, he saw Narcisa playing the leading role in a farce. She caught his eye. After the show was over, the group from Falca was on its way home, walking around the foot of the mountains and joking so as not to feel the steep slopes and the time passing by.

"Neighbour Narcisa, you seem very different when you're acting from what you really are like. I enjoyed seeing you. I spent the whole night looking at you!" said Crisóstomo, the emigrant from South Africa.

"Why do you say what you don't feel?"

"I can prove that I'm not lying."

And as they were in front, lighting their way with a bull's eye lantern, some distance from the group with the other lantern, Crisóstomo said again, "I can prove it to you."

"Tell me how."

"You won't be angry?"

"Why?"

"Listen, Narcisa, I came back from South Africa with the idea of marrying a girl from our village. I like you."

Crisóstomo went back to Johannesburg and a year later Narcisa married him by proxy. Teacher Jorge lost the soul of his theatre, the nights of enchantment, and the nights when the village of Igreja vibrated from the hot breath of the people.

CHAPTER XVII

The tiny world of Achada do Castanheiro, a microcosm, as backward as other places in the rudimentary life of the Island, and thousands of other obscure corners of the earth, continued to be tied to the laws of nature that ruled its very existence. The earth is the greenhouse of life, of lives that are dragged along by virtual ideas of wellbeing, that only emigration can bring. First Artur left and then Francisco and his family.

Inês's parents stayed behind, trying to cultivate the fields and the cow. And weeding, digging, broadcasting the seed, pruning the vines, which they took care of as part of their everyday chores. It was more work but they got more out of it. When they looked at their daughter's house, they were saddened by the sight of the shuttered windows and when night fell on the mountains behind the snow field, they turned to look at the kitchen where, as it grew dark around dinnertime, the smoke from the wood fire that burned on the hearthstones escaped through the holes in the wall and brought some life to the place.

The voice of reason told them silently that Inês was acting sensibly going to join her husband and taking the children. They were trying their luck. And they asked Sta. Quitéria to protect them because they deserved it.

***

While in Achada life was like it was when the island was first inhabited, over in Venezuela a little four room house was sheltering the emigrants. Francisco's bakery was doing well. And after his wife came to help him by serving behind the counter, being served quickly helped to build up their clientele. It didn't take her many weeks of practice to understand the pronunciation and the turns of speech of Venezuelan Spanish. And because she was naturally friendly, almost everyone in the neighbourhood liked her. They didn't call her a foreigner, but a "new Venezuelan".

And so, Inês, who had a gift for persuasion and was good at being sociable, used her talent for perspicacity and talked to everyone but selected those she considered to be worthy of respect and have a good status. At the weekends, they met up with a family from Porto that had come to Caracas in the '40s and was doing very well in industry as they had a plastics factory. From time to time they went out in a Mercedes to the outlying areas. The Pereira's had a daughter who was at high school. Inês took it all in. Anxious for her family to lose the habits learned from generations of living in Achada, she registered her younger children in high school and Carolina in college.

Meanwhile, Francisco, who saw that his wife had a sixth sense that was sharper than other people's, a special gift for presentiment and seeing far ahead, blindly followed her advice. The shop in Achada had failed. She had already known this at the end of the third month. When she arrived in Venezuela, the way she had examined the shop and the impetus that she gave to it had resulted in the development of the making and selling of bread. Inês was the brains and Francisco the brawn. But he tried very hard to give himself an enviable position in the industry he had chosen. At first he had spent night after sleepless night while getting used to it. Fortune had smiled on him as he had an experienced, practical and honest employee who gave him advice. This did not mean, however, that he did not suffer in silence but this suffering had nothing to do with the sacrifices he made. He remembered the revolution that was fought on the streets. He had hidden under a bridge to save himself from being killed and he found some other fugitives sleeping there. The scene of a woman holding on to a baby, who had to be her son, appalled him because of the expression of suffering on their faces as the tears rolled down their sunken cheeks. He spent hours at night listening to the shots. The image still came to him of dying in a strange land far away from home. In the early morning, when he could see dawn coming, the shots faded away in the distance. He came out from under the bridge and keeping close to the walls of the buildings he went down an alley and, without knowing where he was, he went in the direction of his little house. A hundred metres away the little square with the leafy tree was full of people gawking: watching the results of the revolt.

***

Inês furnished her new house in the same taste as Mrs. Pereira, her best friend, with furniture that showed to perfection the favourite style of someone who had always lived in harmony with the lines of utilitarian things, the tangible beauty that delights the eye, not forgetting the carpets and curtains. And on Saturdays they alternated between the Pereira's going to Francisco and Inês's house and their going to the Pereira's. From these friendly reunions, Inês picked up the customs of society that she so much wanted and at the same time a wardrobe from the dressmakers to high society.

One Saturday evening at the Pereira's house, while the men sat in their armchairs chatting about the fortunes of the Portuguese, which had been achieved through intelligence and channelled through the force of will and, often, with strenuous effort, the women chattered about fashion. The young people talked about school, criticising the theories that went in to decorate their memories and never came back out again.

"You know, Mr. Francisco, you came at the right time. Venezuela is developing her immense resources. Anyone who has the will can make a fortune."

"I was lucky but my hard work can't be compared to yours, Mr. Pereira."

You know, small businesses have an advantage over big ones. You have fewer worries and the profits are cleaner."

"Do you intend to stay in Caracas with your family and not go back to Portugal?"

"As you know, my factory is growing. I watched it start and I've watched it grow. I can't turn my back on the future."

"I think differently, Mr. Pereira. If I can manage to put the amount I have in mind in the bank, I'll go home."

"Mr. Francisco, home should be where one makes one's fortune!"

After drinking a mouthful of beer, Francisco replied, "For the money, that's true."

Meanwhile, next to the blood-red mahogany bookcase, filled with luxuriously bound volumes with gilded spines, Armando Pereira and Carolina were flirting, after he had given her Eça de Queirós' book, *The Correspondence of Fradique Mendes*.

"You surely know it?"

"No, I've never read it."

"Well then, read this letter. Or, better still, these passages, and you'll see that I'm Fradique. And you are Clara. The first time that I saw you here in our house, I felt just the same as Fradique."

And she read it with emotion, while Armando leafed through the poems of Rosalia de Castro.

"I passed by, but then everything around seemed to be irrevocably disagreeable and ugly and I turned round to admire her again, to "meditate" in silence on her beauty, that captivated me by its obvious, comprehensible splendour and something, I don't know what, fine, spiritual, painful and bewitching that shone through her and came from her soul. And so intensely was I lost in this contemplation that I took away her image, decorated and entire, without forgetting one lock of her hair or one fold in the silk dress that she wore..."

"That is so romantic!"

"Don't you like it?"

"Like it... I liked it a lot."

"And don't you believe in Fradique?'

"So you want to confess that you're in love with me, Armando?"

"Believe me, Carolina, it was last Saturday, at your house, that I realised the boundless affection that I feel for you, as though years had gone by."

"But you must remember that one day I'll have to go away..."

"What has that to do with it? We'll get married and travel. I'll get to know your land and you'll get to know mine."

For a few moments she was silent, thinking about the past in Achada do Castanheiro. And the pictures jostled each other, all dripping with melancholy. Living in such a rustic, uncultured, poor place. The times when she was a little girl and helped her mother in the shop. That day when she went over the Torrinhas mountains and back with her mother. The poor little house with the kitchen looking onto the street, full of smoke that made your eyes burn and water, the smoke from the vines and the firewood from the mountains that her mother put between the stones on the hearth. And her simple family, her grandparents, poor things, with the rustic customs of their own grandparents. It was a past that she could not forget. A past that was in her blood.

When she came out of her momentary reverie, she said, "I have to confess, Armando, I liked you as soon as I saw you."

And she told him in detail about Achada do Castanheiro where she had been born.

Armando, moved by the sincerity of her autobiography, a sincere confession that showed the purity of her sentiments, told her that his mother, who was now in the high society of Caracas, had also had a humble childhood outside Porto.

"Carolina, we are all born equal. Work and actions are what give people dignity. Nobility is a question of moral and intellectual qualities."

In fact, Armando Pereira was fascinated by Inês's daughter. She was a tall, thin girl with blonde hair and brown eyes. With a sharp intellect, she was interested in the ideas in some books on philosophy. Sociology, in which she was specialising, occupied her attention many hours of the night.

***

When they were back at home, Carolina could not stop herself from telling her mother, just as the damsels did in the "courts of love" in the Middle Ages. She had to share her secret with her. So, before going to bed, she called her mother into her room and sitting together on the edge of the bed, she told her, "Mother, Armando gave me a book and told me that he's loved me since the first day he saw me. I was amazed because I never thought that about him, although I really like him."

"And what did you say?"

"That I loved him too."

"I'm very happy, Carolina! For you to make a good marriage was one of my dearest wishes. Your parents gave you a lesson. You deserve a young man of substance and even riches and you couldn't have found a better one. He's the son of our best friends!"

***

Inês could not sleep that night. She had never imagined that Armando, an engineer, would marry Carolina. She was delighted. And so delightful was this glimpse into the near future that she was living it in the present, a present with no past because it was just imaginary.

Digging among her memories, she remembered her parents in Achada, so simple and honest, and what they would do when they heard about their granddaughter's wedding. How their hearts would leap. And Matilde, Carolina's godmother, would also have to rejoice to see her goddaughter in high society and well married. Only in the morning, when she felt Francisco wake up, did she tell him about Carolina's engagement. He did not find it at all strange since she had had an education.

***

The activity of Francisco's bakery grew considerably after the exchange of ideas on business on those Saturday evenings. When he heard that a bakery in the centre was closing because of a disagreement between the partners, he took Inês's advice and went to see his friend Pereira. They talked at length about the advantages and the obstacles that could come about if he took the opportunity to buy it.

"Mr. Pereira, how can I find out about how things are with the partners? I'm still a stranger here and I don't know any people that are in that business."

"My friend, I'll take care of it. Let's talk again the day after tomorrow."

And, as agreed, they met and Pereira told Francisco about the problem at the company. The question was simple to summarize: two partners, both dishonest, had embezzled a large amount of money and run off to Argentina. The other two could not agree: the bakery was closing. They were selling the equipment and the owner of the premises was renting it out for the same business or one similar.

Pereira acted as the go-between for the Portuguese buyer with the interested parties. After the deeds had been signed, it was not many days before the factory had the workers it needed and normal operations began. In spite of the large outlay, the profit made it worth it. The family from Achada was beginning to be talked about in the financial world because of its solidity.

Francisco Freitas did not end his old habits of getting up early in the morning that he had had back in the rural hamlet of his humble childhood among the humble clover, when he had got out of bed to take a bunch of grass to the calf. Now he got up early to go to the garage, get into the car, look over his recently acquired factory and then spend his time in the office where his son checked the accounts in his free time after school.

One afternoon, when he stopped at the office door, looking out at the noisy, busy life on the street, feeling a euphoria inside because of the pleasure this gave to his eyes and because of his financial independence, a boy, whose face and clothes showed he was an immigrant, came up to him. He half recognised him. The newcomer raised his hand to his hat, an old fashioned felt one of indeterminate colour, and greeted him.

"Good afternoon, Mr. Francisco. You don't recognise me. That's natural. Time passes. It's been many years!"

Puzzled, he looked at him and began to recognise him; now he was a man and in his memory was a picture of a child, but his eyes still had the same sparkle. Francisco smiled, remembering him and placing him in time and space.

"If it isn't Jorge, Ratazana's son, an urchin who was always up to mischief."

"That's me, yes, sir!"

"And how come you're here?"

"I asked the vicar for some money and told him I had to leave."

"What did you do back there in Achada?"

"Day labouring, and, in the end sometimes without a penny in my pocket. Mr. Francisco knows what life is like in the country for someone like me!"

"Are you still single?"

"No, sir, I married Parruca's granddaughter."

"Did you bring her with you?"

"Yes, sir."

"But you couldn't know I was here!"

"No, sir. I had your address, I mean, the address of your house, but when I was coming down this street, I looked at this bakery and at you and then I recognised you."

"Who gave you my address?"

"It was your mother in law!"

"Is she doing well?"

"I should say so! She has the land and the family is small."

"Do you have a job?"

"No, sir. I came looking for you to see if you could find me a job."

"Ok, Jorge. You can work in my factory."

"Oh! Thank you, sir. How can I repay this great favour?"

"By working willingly."

And so Ratazana's son, the one who had gone to Francisco Freitas' barn when he was a boy and cut the tail off the calf, started working in Caracas.

CHAPTER XVIII

Inês learned of her husband's generous gesture at dinner. He told her how he had been disconcerted by the unexpected appearance of Jorge Ratazana at the office door. She was happy that Francisco had held out a hand to help a compatriot who was as isolated from the good things of life. As a child, Ratazana's poor son had been left to himself, receiving no healthy paternal instruction, until he was fourteen and studied with Teacher Jorge.

Ratazana soon adapted to his new job at the bakery and was hardworking, punctual and obedient. The Islander, as the Portuguese and some of the Venezuelans among his co-workers nicknamed him, never spoke about his boss except as Mr. Francisco Freitas. Somewhere in a dark corner of his memory, he remembered the evil deed that he had done to his benefactor long ago. That evil deed made Jorge hold the man who was now his support in a foreign land in the highest esteem. Without anyone guessing it, and without his realising himself, he became a kind of secret agent in the factory. This was confirmed when the workers tried to go on strike. By chance, Jorge heard a group of them talking at lunchtime about how they were not satisfied with the wages, although they had agreed to the increase in a meeting and told the management so. That same day, Ratazana's son went to Francisco Freitas' house. After going down side streets, avoiding the cars, as light footed as if he was walking along the paths in Achada, not noticing the time passing by or hearing the noise from a shop, he knocked on the door, after the checking the number to be sure it was the right house. It was Francisco himself who opened the door, after looking out from the veranda to see who it was.

"What's happening, Jorge? Do you need something?"

And Jorge told him all that he had heard from that small group and described the three men, whom he did not know well.

Having been warned, Francisco put a stop to the little rebellion. He was grateful to Jorge and transferred him to an easier job with greater responsibility and higher wages.

***

Although it is certain that she was now moving in different circles, Inês's love for her parents was still there, like the sacred flame in the temple of Venus. She never let a month pass by without writing to them. In one of her letters she said:

"Dear father and mother,

"At Christmas it will be twelve years since I last saw you. I miss you seeing you and hugging you and I remember our poor little house. We are all well.
"Carolina is going to marry a young man from Porto who is an engineer. Anabela will become a doctor this year and Carlos will be a lawyer. Francisco has been working very hard. Thanks be to God and Sta. Quitéria; the business is doing as well as I hoped. Sometime soon we will be coming home for ever."
"I forgot to say that the money from the cheque is for father to buy a suit and mother a dress. Whatever is left over, use it to buy better food."

The memory of her friend Matilde was also as fresh in Inês's mind as that faraway day when they said goodbye on the dock. She still felt the same sisterly affection and incredible admiration for her and it was no pretence. Her heart was so naturally pure and her affection so unblemished that it was spontaneously given to whoever shared her friendship, which was as clear as the water in the gullies in Achada. Hypocrisy and material interest played no part in her affection for those who shared the same spirit as her simple but noble nature.

Never a year went by that Inês did not send her friend Matilde a small gift by post or with someone from Madeira who was going home for good or to visit the family. The last time it had been a pretty silk scarf with a fringe. Her *comadre* always told her how thankful she was and how much she missed her, and Carolina, her brother and sister and Francisco.

"Inês,

"I was so grateful for your gift, as so often before, and especially because you don't forget our friendship. If my husband comes back from Antigua in August, I'll come to my goddaughter's wedding. I'll be very happy to make the journey. I miss all of you very much.
    "Kisses from your friend and comadre,
    "Matilde"

***

About the time Francisco was setting himself up in the bakery, the property that Artur had sold, which was about 80 hectares, changed ownership: Gregório, the son of Bajeca, bought it. He had inherited his father's knack for fraudulent business deals. He came from Brazil with only a few cruzeiros but enough to become the owner of Artur's old farm.

His trade as an immigrant was dealing in cattle. He boasted of his talent for picking out the best cattle and horses. And the farmers round about took this for granted. His fame had increased since the day at an Italian's farm when they had bet two thousand bolivars on the person who could tell which was the Brazilian creole and which the Argentinean horse. The two dealers waved their arms and became very animated, until Gregório came out of his silence, asked permission to give his opinion and said,

"This one" – pointing at the closest one – is the Brazilian creole because it's more powerful. That's the Argentinean. Look, it's lighter."

And Bajeca's son won two thousand bolivars.

He had fifteen cows on the farm. Around Christmas, a man from Madeira, from Calheta, came to buy a cow. Gregório showed him one of the better ones. When he separated her from the others in the corral, she started to run. So Bajeca tied a rope around its horns and immediately tied the rope round a tree. He changed the price of the animal and the deal was done. The money was crackling in his trouser pocket where he had put it and the cow went off with her new owner.

He was living with his guard dog, Tiger, in a little house with a tin roof. For how long? He had inherited the same nomadic, vagabond instincts that his father had picked up when he immigrated to Brazil. First he was in Carabolo dealing in cattle and horses. Then he was in the Federal District. Till when? He was accused of killing two puppies that belonged to another farmer three kilometres away under cover of night. He found out that a certain Guilherme had spread the rumour. He jumped up and went off like a madman in search of him. He found him in a neighbour's yard where he was looking after the oxen.

"Was I the one who killed those puppies? You liar!"

And without listening to the other man's defence, he punched him in the nose. Blood ran out. Guilherme shouted out but only the echoes answered.

Around that time, Bajeca had made a good deal with some cattle for slaughter and he went off to the capital to enjoy himself in his own bohemian way. It was election time and he did not know how dangerous a risk he was taking going out on the streets at night. As he was going round a huge tree to go into a wide cross street, a policeman went up to him and asked what he was doing. He walked on without replying as if he had not heard the question, which was repeated. It was this indifference to authority that earned him a blow on the arm from the policeman's club. Unable to stand the pain, he jumped at the policeman and bit him. Another policeman appeared and they arrested him and took him to a dark room where he spent the night.

They let him go as day came and Man went back to his millennial battle to survive.

Angrily, he remembered Lombada, where he had been born. He could not explain why he felt such an attraction at that moment for his old mud brick house with the sagging tile roof and so hated being away. That feeling of repulsion was heightened by his nostalgia and little by little it seeped into the back of his memory.

A night of dissipation with whores and a sleepless night in jail had punished his thirty-five year old body. He thought about this as he sat on the seat of the train that was taking him to the interior. It wasn't that he wasn't in the prime of life but this was a mountebank's life. His stomach dictated when it was time for lunch and dinner. And it was a barmaid in a flea-bitten tavern, with her hair falling into the dish, who almost always served him either at the counter or at a rickety table.

His father did not want to go with him because he preferred to stay with the Spanish woman who rented him a room near the farm, rather than go with him so that they could help each other.

Out of the cattle dealing, he earned enough to buy clothes and shoes and there was even enough to spend on leading a fast life in whichever city he wanted to. But he would never be thirty again.

When he got to the farm, a cattle buyer was waiting for him. It was José Fernandez from Caniço, who had come on behalf of his father-in-law to get a Zebu bull.

"I have a Zebu but he's pretty wild."

"I want it to be a Zebu. My father-in-law has it in mind to have the leather tanned for some customers."

"I'll see if I can rope him, because he is wild, as I already told you."

"Let's see if he gets away!"

The manoeuvre was hard but Gregório had had lots of practice. He never feared having to catch a bullock. But when he threw the rope and was pulling on it, the Zebu kicked him in the face so hard that he fell down unconscious. When he opened his eyes, he was horrified to see that he was in bed. His head and face hurt. Seated on a wooden bench at his side, the tavern keeper was looking at him unfeelingly. Gregório saw from her expression that she was bored and anxious to get away.

"Do you feel better?"

"Yes, but it hurts."

"Your face is really swollen!"

"Can you get me a glass of milk? I'll pay you for your time."

"I'll go and see if I can get some quickly as I can't leave the shop with the kid."

And she left hurriedly.

Left alone, he looked at the blank walls of the room and as there was nothing to see, he tired of looking. He turned over. He couldn't see anything. Not even the bare walls of the stable. He went from looking to thinking. He thought about how unhappy he was at thirty-five years old. Over there, he didn't have a mother's or a sister's or a relative's love. The barmaid's unwillingness, as if he were a grumpy old man, and the disdain with which she had looked at him made him feel even more alone. Is it because the women from Beira are unlovely and uncharitable? They were both emigrants. No feeling born of a clash between the races separated them. But he felt that he had no family.

He reacted to his sickly state. This drooping feeling must have been caused by the blow. And because it didn't go away, he went out into the street. When he got to the tavern, he the glass of milk was still not ready. The barmaid was surprised to see him. When she saw him, she exclaimed,

"I was just going over there!"

Back at home, he went to get the bullock. He took the Zebu to José Fernandez, and, like his father before him, he began to say that one of his bullocks had disappeared. It had been robbed. Who could it be? His suspicions fell on José Fernandez.

***

The weeks went by. There were fewer and fewer cattle deals. Gregório killed a cow from time to time and continued living. But this was not a life for an immigrant.

One Saturday around Easter, Fernandez, who had not yet paid for the Zebu, appeared at Bajeca's farm on horseback. He came up at a trot and then slowed down. He dismounted and held the horse.

"Didn't you trust me?"

"I know that you never intended to owe me, so I was in no doubt about that."

"Well, let's do the arithmetic."

And Fernandez took out his wallet to pay for the Zebu.

Gregório immediately said, "The Zebu and the bullock!"

"The bullock?"

"Yes!"

"But I didn't take any bullock!"

"Oh yes you did!"

"You're not trying to trick me?"

"That one with the black spots that you were praising."

"You're not thinking straight. That kick from the Zebu went to your head."

Knowing that his trick was failing, Gregório then said, "Didn't your father-in-law send someone to get the bullock during that week I was away?"

"I don't think so!"

"Well, let me tell you that someone stole my bullock. And whoever took it knew the lie of the land."

Disappointed by Gregório's insincerity, José Fernandez took the money out of his wallet, placed it on top of a box, untied the horse from the wire fence, mounted and merely said, "Be seeing you!"

And he left at a trot, under the pale, late evening sun.

About the same time, Bajeca received a letter from Caracas from his former boss in Carabolo, telling him that he was interested in talking to Gregório after selling a business. He got ready and went to the city. But he went there too soon. He should not have left the country without finding out if the other man was in Caracas. Because he would only be back the next day from a business trip to one of the other states, Gregório wandered around the streets like a sleepwalker. As he did not have much money, he lay down on a park bench and went to sleep. Late that night, he woke up, got up and wandered around the city. On other benches he saw other men sleeping, as he had. And he thought to himself: I wonder if any of those people are Portuguese, from the Island?

Looking inside cars, he was surprised to see men wrapped in blankets. He decided that everywhere there were people with less luck than his. Including his compatriots.

At nine o'clock next morning he knocked on his old boss's door. Mr. Daniel, his face well shaven and wearing light coloured pyjamas, asked him in.

"So, you came today?"

"No. Yesterday."

"Where did you sleep?"

"On a park bench."

"So you did the same as other immigrants... When you were here yesterday, why didn't you say that you didn't have anywhere to sleep?"

"I didn't want to bother you..."

"So, the cat got your tongue. It costs nothing to ask."

"But I slept well outside."

"That's not surprising. Others do the same when they don't have a home. Now, tell me, do you want to work in a factory?"

"What kind of factory?"

"A dye works."

"And what do I do with my business?"

"Sell it. There's always someone interested in living away from the city, however badly."

"But in a factory, I wouldn't be a free man."

"Isn't it better to earn a wage you can count on?"

"And when I go home, I'll have empty pockets."

"Yes, if you spend it all!"

And so Gregório listened to his old boss, his friend, and started working in the factory. There, he had a smoother life, although he didn't like saving. It wasn't in his blood. He was one of the many people for whom a foreign land is their stepmother, because they want it to be. Save money? No. It came in with the tide and went out with it again.

Bajeca senior found out that his son was working in a factory. He asked around and heard from his pals that he could catch him when the workers left the factory.

Abruptly he said, "Gregório, what about your cattle business?"

"I'm going to sell it."

"No. I'll take it over and I'll give you your share of the profits."

So, Bajeca took over the farm. He lived alone. He gave up his woman, who had started to mistreat him because he had spent everything: what he'd earned from his wanderings and what she had worked hard to get and hidden as her nest egg. He went to the surrounding villages looking for deals, preferably in Zebu cattle. As he was used to being dishonest in all sales and exchanges, he was making a living but not prospering. One sleepless night, he looked back at the past and wondered about the future. What would happen when his muscles stiffened up and his face was all wrinkled? After examining his conscience, he decided to go back to his wife. Hiding his plan from his son, he sold the farm and with the money he legally paid off a large debt for some cattle to an Italian, went back to Rio de Janeiro, dressed himself to the nines, bought a fibre suitcase, went to a travel agency and sailed back to the Island looking like a rich man.

Bajeca's biography soon went the rounds. The son was always a better man than the father. He wrote to his mother to tell her of his father's ingratitude in selling the business that had cost him so many misfortunes. But he did not want anything bad to happen to his father. May God give him good health.

Back home, with a coiled rope hanging off his shoulder. Bajeca soon adapted to the primitive life of raising cattle. Afterwards, sitting by the barn door, he went over the life he had undone by emigrating and having bad luck. So many years in Brazil and Venezuela, cheating this one and that one, sorry for having split open the head of the husband of the woman who helped to keep him alive with a pruning hook.

"Everyone has a destiny," he would say to those who asked him ironically which bank he kept his bolivars and cruzeiros in. And with bitterness etched on his face, shaking his head, he would end every conversation with, "Being born was the worst thing that happened to me!"

CHAPTER XIX

One Saturday, the Pereira family came to Francisco Freitas' house. Moments before the coffee came, Mrs. Maria Pereira told Inês in very confidential tones that Armando wished to marry Carolina.

As they sat chatting together on the sofa in friendly fashion, Maria Pereira said to her friend, "My Armando has found the girl of his dreams in Carolina. You know very well what my son's qualities are."

"And you know Carolina. You know that she has gifts that are rare in girls in society today. And it's not only her manner but also her independence, which made her study."

Inês was at her happiest, with feelings that she had never experienced before. Such was her joy that her eyes were shining brighter than usual, showing the emotions that were making her heart pound.

While Armando and Carolina were looking through an album of postcards from Madeira, Francisco Freitas and Fonseca Pereira rarely changed the subject. Business was their normal topic of conversation and everyday activities were in all their turns of phrase. If by chance the conversation took a detour into some political or social problem, it always went back to their ideas about factory production. Mr. Fonseca Pereira explained how to advertise plastics by using practical psychology: illuminated signs with pictures that made it unnecessary to show the name of the company. The public loved distractions, and although it was unnecessary, the truth was that advertising was always advertising!

Francisco Freitas did not forget to mention how well his factory was doing and the attempt to call a strike, which had not succeeded because of the cleverness of one of his compatriots who played the part of a secret agent.

And so they talked on. Meanwhile, Carolina was showing Armando pictures of the interior of the Island and a postcard showing the bonfire on St. Sylvester's night. He was enchanted by the picture and because of the natural enthusiasm of their mutual affection, he said, in an uncontrollable emotional outburst,

"I want to get to know your land, Carolina! It must be one of the wonders of the modern world."

"Do you think so?"

"Why not? If the Greeks could have seven of the wonders of the world, out of all the works of art planned and built by Man, why shouldn't there be a creation that Nature has given us, a wonder of the natural world?"

"You're right. It's not one of Man's works but a divine creation."

"I believe in metaphysics too. But, Carolina, because we live on sensations, I've already made my plans. Let's get married this year and our first trip will be to your island."

"If you want!"

"I feel such a desire to see the country where you were born! Without you, my life would have no purpose, believe me."

And so, because of the tender ideas, experiences and feelings that they exchanged, harmony decided everything, a unity of ideas and sentiments.

"Mr. Francisco, you and your family's coming here as immigrants has brought my family more happiness than I can say. We know a lot of people, but out of all of them, my friend, your wife and children have become like members of our family. And now, with Armando marrying Carolina, that friendship is going to be even closer, if that's possible."

"But is it a certainty? It gives me such great happiness that I find it hard to believe."

"Well, it's true, my friend."

"So, Mr. Pereira, let me give you an embrace."

Standing up, they held each other close for a long time.

"What's happening?" asked Inês, surprised by the scene.

"It's about the happiness of our daughter."

"And of our son," interrupted Maria Pereira.

And so, that evening, the marriage between Carolina and Armando became a fact.

***

Jorge Ratazana saved enough after his daily household expenses to put a few bolivars in the bank. He led a quiet life, going from his home to the factory and from the factory to his home. When he went home in the evening, the uproar in the crowded streets always appalled him because he remembered the contrast with the quiet life in Achada, the Easter sunsets when the voices of the groups of young people rang through the village as they returned from the Novenas. And then the voices died away as the little groups split up at the entrance to Achada and in front of the houses.

He never showed any tendency to be a womanizer. He did notice, in that foreign land, that many women with sharp eyes got inside a man. And he said to himself that the eyes of some of them were like glass, shining like mirrors do when a ray of sunshine hits them.

As he was leaving work after some months working as a baker, he noticed a stout Venezuelan woman with coal black hair who looked at him with blazing eyes that made his insides boil. She was waiting for her husband, an Italian, on the corner of the street about two metres from the door that he would come out of when he left work. Jorge became curious and watched her as she waited, every day except Wednesday, which was her husband's day off, when there were no eyes looking at him, either from the corner or nearby. The husband, who was short and skinny, was an obvious contrast to his wife. Jorge watched a comic episode one breezy, rainy afternoon. She had her umbrella up and when another passerby, who was also carrying an umbrella, passed by, the two umbrellas became entangled. They were insulting each other at the very moment when the husband came out. Not knowing the reason for the argument, he was convinced that the man had been harassing his wife. He punched him, the police came, and soon there was a horde of gawkers around them. After the reason was explained, the Italian apologized, embarrassed by his aggression, and did not go to jail because the man with the umbrella forgave him.

That afternoon of that sudden, public farce, Jorge felt that the plan that his ardent imagination had built up, to possess the woman, had been ruined.

The scene, the gestures and certain words whose meaning he understood dampened his enthusiasm, his bewitchment, losing his head as if he were eighteen years old over a woman who had seemed different from the many who went down the street on their way home from work. And because he still remembered spending his youth with his sweethearts from his village, he could still feel the heat of their hands in his, the softness of their skin that, with no effort on his part, conjured up a desire to touch and fondle all the skin that was hidden. His memory showed him the life that he had lived and never finished. This was why his lips retained forever a memory of the thing that has life, the softness of a virgin's mouth, that of his neighbour from Cabo da Rabeira, who used to cut grass with him between the vines.

So he went up the street, avoiding those who were coming toward him, and memories of his youth rose up in his imagination, like air bubbles rising and breaking on top of spring water.

And he remembered courting the woman who was waiting at home for him, with no one else to count on.

Walking along the street, he wondered why he had no enthusiasm for the woman who had made his head spin when he was eighteen. The memory of her soft hands passed before his eyes, but it brought no joy. Why did the memory of those first kisses fade? Because youth had gone! That couldn't be it, could it? Hadn't the Spanish woman turned his head? He had desired her fiercely. But when he stopped to think about his own thoughts, the attraction that he had felt for the Spanish woman did not compare with how he had felt when young. Long ago, and becoming longer every year, back there in Achada, where a long time was still a long time because memories have a time that is not based on people or things, his love was more than physical. But why did possessing a body change love and make it cease to exist? The girl who had made him crazy was waiting for him back home. Did he only see the body of the Spanish woman now? Why didn't his wife awaken the same interest now as she had when he met her, with the enthusiasm of romantic love, far away in time and space?

CHAPTER XX

Why had he emigrated? And if he hadn't, instead of the Spanish woman, would some other woman have turned his head?

He wandered around, thinking that the streets seemed shorter. He looked for a clock. In the end he had spent more time walking than usual. The walks helped him to think and remember.

Rosa had taken the pot off the stove as it was already over cooked and burnt.

"You came home so late!"

"It always takes the same time to walk it."

"No, today you were later. And I was getting upset."

Jorge told her in detail about the scene he had witnessed.

"But you knew I was here alone waiting for you, upset, without being able to go looking for you."

"Don't get upset. If I came home later than usual, it's because of what I told you."

"Listen, Jorge, I'm sorry I left our little house in Achada."

"Why?"

"I was happy there. I was never alone. If you were late, I'd go to my mother's house, when she didn't come to ours. And then there were the nephews, the neighbours coming in to borrow a stick of firewood when they didn't have any. I was never alone."

"But you were satisfied!"

"I was at the beginning. Now I want to be at home. I don't understand these people. And I'm alone, always alone, always waiting for you to come home."

"We're not going to stay here for the rest of our lives!"

"I hope not!"

"The years will pass by fast and we'll go back with some money."

"Oh yes. But I want to be in Achada. Get rich, why? We don't have any children!"

"We can't complain. Give it time, Rosa!"

"Ay! Emigrate! Emigrate! What for? For this! To live at the end of the world!"

Rosa had got all that she felt off her chest. Inside, her husband agreed with her.

After a few days had passed, Jorge said hello to the Spanish woman and received a complacent smile in return.

One evening, as soon as she saw Jorge, she smiled at him and went round the corner of the building. Intuitively understanding her gesture, he followed her from afar, on the other side of the road. They exchanged hot glances that spoke of possessing a desired object. And they spoke to each other.

That evening, Rosa wept. Her husband was even later than the day before.

"You're drifting away from me!"

Jorge begged her forgiveness. He had more work. There was more to do every day.

"I curse the day I left home," said Rosa, her voice husky with sobs.

"Don't worry. I'll come home earlier."

It was a Friday. Jorge asked Francisco Freitas if he could take some time off after lunch because his wife was ill. The Spanish woman, as they had arranged, was looking impatiently at her wrist watch. Her sharp hearing, waiting for the slightest noise, noted that someone had stopped by the door. The key turned. The door opened and shut. And there in the simply furnished bedroom, where an olive green curtain covered the door that led to the tiny corridor, they sat down on the edge of the bed arm in arm. He looked into her eyes, which were like a magnet. His arm fell and his hand felt the hardness and the heat of the leg, which had the same quality as the eyes.

Carried away by the ecstasy that only sensibility can transmit and the senses can live, as if there were no other world than oneself, another self came into the lovers' world: the husband, a driver. He had forgotten his watch and he could not travel without it, like a windmill with no wind. He was a rigid man. Not a minute later or a minute earlier at work, when travelling and even in his conversation. For him, time was an obsession. Except at home.

When he suddenly saw his wife with a man who was not hers (the enormity of it drove him to that conclusion) he became enraged. He picked up the chair that was at the foot of the bed and began to hit both the adulteress and Jorge with it, relentlessly. Jorge was wounded on the head by a chair leg. The blood ran down his face from the hard blow. Stunned, he fell down. While the woman was defending herself with a pillow, Jorge took his chance and ran out of the room. He had to get to safety, through the front door, which was standing open. A passerby, struck by the man's appearance, took him to the hospital where the doctors looked at him.

After treating the wound, which took some time, they would not let him go home until the next day. Worried about how his wife would feel not knowing what had happened to him, anxiously wondering at his absence, thinking that he had lost his life in some accident, Jorge had an idea. What if he phoned Francisco Freitas? And this immediately made his compatriot and employer go to see him, when he was surprised by the news and heard the trembling voice of Ratazana.

In a few minutes, the car took him to the hospital.

"So, what happened?"

And Jorge told him, in detail, about his unfortunate amorous adventure. After finding out about the treatment and the patient's state, Francisco Freitas got permission to take him home. He was sad for Ratazana, with a kind of pity for his harebrained mind and even for the uproar he had caused in Achada, which had done little harm but had made the neighbours shout at him. Also, he had not forgotten how dedicated he was to him as an employee at the factory. So, he put Jorge in his car and took him home. Shouting and swearing, Perruca's granddaughter threw her arms around her husband and cursed the day that they had left home. Francisco Freitas calmed her down by saying that no one could avoid having an accident in the street even if they were careful of the traffic.

"The traffic makes people blind, Rosinha! In a few days Jorge will be better and more cautious."

And, in fact, it did him good, as Jorge Ratazana never forgot that lesson from his first days as an immigrant.

CHAPTER XXI

Thirty-five years of a wearisome life and nights with little or no sleep had made Artur grow old, making the legacy of those last years in Caracas, when he had lived with that Spanish woman, even worse. She had worn him down because after he neglected her, she could not bear his disdain and stuck to him like a limpet to a rock. And the butcher's shop was not doing well.

He did not feel like continuing the hard fight or dying on the outskirts of the city far from his family. He had burned up the strength in his muscles in the butcher's shop, his youth had gone, and he was like a pine tree that had been burned in a fire. It was over thirty years since he had heard any news of his wife and children. The woman from Bahia, the Spanish woman and the others had driven out his love for Maria Clara and he was no longer the homesick Artur who at times was sorry that he had left Achada and wanted his wife while he was having an affair with that accursed woman from Bahia. Now he decided to go home, whatever happened. He would sell the business. One night at a party at the house of the Freitas brothers from Campanário, they proposed that he sell them the butcher's shop. He thought about it carefully. The mother of his sons was worth more than any number of women from Bahia or Spain. They wanted to suck him dry like leaches do when they latch onto a sick person's skin. It was true that everything happened while he was working so, in spite of everything, he had managed to put a little money in the bank.

The days went by slowly, at more of a snail's pace than before. He had never felt that time rushed to the weekends when he was in a strange land; the weeks seemed endless. His desire to go back to Achada robbed him of his sleep and the nights were endless too.

One Saturday, as evening fell, he got into his car and drove off, as fearful as ever of having an accident, never pressing down on the accelerator to go at more than 70 kilometres an hour, to the edge of the city and the Freitas brothers' house. The light was fading. He got out, locked the car door and took in a bottle of champagne. He received an exuberant welcome.

"So, what about our deal?" asked the older Freitas brother immediately.

"How much will you give me for everything?"

"Thirty thousand escudos."

"I accept. Deal's done. Word of honour."

"We'll give you the money tomorrow."

And after an evening of talking about their villages, the pig killing parties around Christmas, the happiness of the "Birth Masses", the family, the merriment when they were youngsters, the sweethearts, and the bitter moments, the irremediable sadness when they wanted to buy a new suit and their father didn't have any money, the older Freitas said,

"I was twelve years old. My father had a little patch of reedy land that hardly produced enough for the family. When December was coming, I used to complain almost every day at lunch that I didn't have a suit for the holidays. My father couldn't afford one. I can see now that he really wanted to buy me one and I believe that he just couldn't. I'm sorry now. But I didn't let up on my father. 'I don't have a suit for the holidays!' And my mother used to say to me, with tears in her eyes, 'Son, we just can't. Get used to it.' Life was like that, Mr. Artur, and that's still the life of the majority of those who live in Campanário. There's no water on the land in many parts. They've only got what the land gives to eat. There are no jobs. Digging is hard work. Look, if I didn't sometimes send my parents something, what would happen to them? It was a good thing that my brother and I came over here. We work. We're out of poverty. We want a thousand, two thousand... it's easier than getting someone over there in the parish to lend you a hundred escudos. But I must confess that if we are doing well today, we mustn't forget Dr. Paulino from Serra d'Água who lent us the money. He's a good doctor and a good friend. Now, Mr. Artur, you're going to take him a shirt and tie to remember us by."

The following day, after the deal was done, Artur put the money into his wallet, and as it was already eight o'clock at night, he went to the beer bar where he got into an animated conversation with some Portuguese from the continent and from his island. And they drank some beer.

"In two weeks' time I hope to go home," said Artur.

"I don't yet know when that day will come. Business has been bad," said Ireneu from Ponta do Pargo.

Well, I sold my butcher's shop and here's the money." And with his right hand he touched his left hand coat pocket.

"You have all the luck, Mr. Artur! You're going to go back to the family and take them out of mourning, said Figueira from Caniço.

"It's more than time. It's been thirty years since I left home."

"So you have a nice fortune," said Figueira.

"I could have had one, I could! But a man only sees what's there. He only sees other women and loses his head. And the money goes away."

"Look here, Mr. Artur, I send them all to hell! There was one who wanted to catch me but I ran with her and nothing more! That was when I'd just got here," said Ireneu.

"I can tell you that we are not all alike," said Artur and, ending the conversation, "It's getting late." And they separated.

Artur went down the street, avoiding the dark corners, with his mind going over the past in a sudden pang of conscience. Figueira was right when he said that he should have a nice fortune. But women were his downfall.

He was deep in thought when a car stopped a few metres in front of him. Two men in masks pointed guns at him, rifled through his pockets and took his wallet. It all happened in the twinkling of an eye and the passersby did not even notice. He was furious. But who could he complain to? He'd lost his money for ever.

He did not sleep that night. He felt incapable of putting off his trip and setting up in business again.

He got up early and a happy thought came into his mind. He still had the car to sell. He would ask the Freitas brothers to buy the car. He went to the bank and took out the ten thousand escudos that he has saved and, without losing any time, he went to the airline office and bought a ticket for the plane from Caracas to Lisbon, for the next day, 16th November. It would be his second journey by air. He had come to Brazil by boat thirty-some years before, an adventure that he would never forget because, with only five hundred escudos in his pocket, apart from the few thousand he had kept back to set up in business, as he was uncertain of finding a job, he had been full of happiness. Who isn't the lord of the universe at thirty-five years old! Mixing with the Italian, Czechoslovakian and Spanish emigrants, he had felt part of a great family in the tourist class on board the *Cape Horn.*

Now he was filled with a fear of flying. But he would not go by sea, just before Christmas. He had to go by air, caged up like someone going to heaven. His greatest wish, which made him nervous, was to get home without his wife knowing. In his imagination, she was busy with the work on the farm, digging the ground, sowing and watering just as on the morning when he left on her way to water the beans over by Lombadinha. A memory of the last hour of water at Levada Grande came into his mind. They went together, one behind the other, up the twisting path to the field. They had been married for three years. But Maria Clara drove him as crazy as if he had just noticed her for the first time. Her eyes were coal black, her face was pretty and her shapely legs were as white as the snow and, when she tucked up her skirt to water the beans, they made him go crazy. The legs of the woman from Bahia were nothing in comparison to his wife's. Looking at them, he always wanted to stroke them and run his hand up over her soft skin. The years went by. In his mind's eye, he saw her as she had been on the morning they said goodbye. They had hugged. "Now I'm going to do the watering," she had said, "You go off to your destiny, with the blessing of God." He had not forgotten those words with the passage of time. Maria Clara had turned twenty-eight the month before he left. Will she be different" he asked himself. He imagined her at that same age, still a young woman. The idea of surprising her delighted him and he felt a little crazy.

The day before he left he wandered around the shops to buy some things for his wife and children. But he still felt a sadness pricking him that something was being left behind: the land that could have made him rich.

The Freitas brothers drove him to airport.

The butcher's shop, with its good clientele, made money for its new owners. They had no employees. The sons took charge of the business. However, one evening at dusk a car drew up outside the door. Three men armed with pistols got out and demanded the money in the safe. Ricardo, one of the older Freitas' sons, feeling that something out of the ordinary was happening, got his pistol, rushed into the shop from the next room and fired at the thieves. One fell down near the counter and the others, disconcerted by the unexpected occurrence, rushed out to the car and disappeared.

That scene was part of life for an immigrant. They earned money but they were intruders and subject to the vagaries of fortune. And the Freitas family from Campanário continued to develop their business, stayed on at the butcher's shop and got to know the faces of the customers, but with their eyes fixed on the millions of bolivars for the journey home.

CHAPTER XXII

Gregório got used to the busy life of the city and the work schedule at Mr. Daniel's factory. Now he didn't have to worry about doing the arithmetic of buying and selling cattle. These were other habits. He got used to living in the city with two other Portuguese men from the North. One was from the outskirts of Viana do Castelo and the other from hills of Barroso.

Daniel, his boss, a man with a good heart, put him up in the garage because he felt sorry for him and his wrongheadedness. An iron bedstead with a bench at the head and a portable washbasin in one corner of the room were all the furniture. Here he would often return almost drunk on beer. He was woken up in the morning by the noise of the people walking by in the street, by the rhythm of their footsteps, and he opened his sleepy eyes and got up because the factory was calling. He lost all hope of saving any bolivars to enjoy resting at home after his strength ran out. One idea was like a drug: the desire to see night fall so he could enjoy drinking the ambrosia, seated at a table with his friends.

His mother, his poor mother, wrote him a pitiful letter in which she talked about her worries. It was three pages long but he had to search for the beginning of the second and third pages as the sheets were not numbered. Out of the handful of news, there was one piece that said he was right to have gone against his mother's wish to see him get married before he emigrated, leaving his wife at home. It was better to go to Brazil as a bachelor. Those who emigrate should be free. And, sounding out the words, he read about the misfortunes in the north of the island. At some point, the letter said:

"Gregório my son the daughter of Ramalho from Faja do Penedo fell off the Rocha path at the foot of the picture of Lord Jesus and she got drunk in Poção and the body was in pieces she

threw herself off where you can see the sea at the bottom and her mother was nagging her to marry a cousin who had gone to Brazil three years before but she was unhappy and a man from Falca got in with her and she got a big belly and was having a baby and she was ashamed and one Sunday morning she left the house and killed herself."

And at the end came her bitterest complaints: his father had come back home with only one suit to wear. And she wanted to know who was going to dig the land for the beans if his father was already old and worn out. He, Gregório, was her only hope. She waited week after week for him to send the money for the new house. And she told him that their neighbour, José Pedreiro, never let a day go by without asking, "When do we start the foundations for the house?"

"My son you are my future as I'm old and tired."

CHAPTER XXIII

Artur arrived at Lisbon airport. Because the city was like a flower with a scent that he had never smelled, he collected his luggage and a taxi driver drove the Venezuelan from Portela. He asked the driver if he knew of a boarding house on a busy, but quiet street not far from the noisier centre of Baixa. He took Artur to the Avenida Duque de Loulé. Because he came from primitive rural surroundings, what impressed him in a strange land was the size of things, so he made comparisons between big things and small things. His eyes became accustomed to measuring the streets and buildings, squares and gardens like an instinctive tape measure.

He liked the city. He thought it was much smaller than Caracas, where there were huge, imposing buildings and wide avenues.

He went out next morning about nine o'clock. The pavements in front of the rows of houses were overflowing with men and women hurrying along, the men dressed in overcoats and carrying umbrellas and the women wrapped up in short jackets and carrying handbags. A cold breeze was blowing in their faces and ruffling their hair. The Venezuelan came out slowly and walked slowly, almost getting in the way of those who were late for work and had to go round this unhurried stroller. One passerby was more impulsive. Brushing his arm, he stared at him and, turning his head, murmured, "What a snail!"

But Artur went on his way, treading the pavement like someone who had spent his whole life sauntering.

Almost at the end of Avenida Duque de Loule, where there was a small square, the streets opened up and on the left he saw a statue with a shape that impressed him. He looked at the plaque and read: Camilo Castelo Branco. The name meant nothing to him. He dug in his memory but his memory had nothing to offer. He turned to his imagination. Was he a politician? A millionaire? He decided that it must be a portrait in stone of an important person. He used this adjective, which can mean anything because of its lack of precision, and his curiosity was satisfied, and then was rekindled by the grandeur of the statue that stands on the Marques de Pombal roundabout. He stood there, looking up, with his mouth wide open, petrified in front of the monument until this feeling was lessened simply by standing there. While he was standing there, perplexed, he heard someone close to him say,

"The statue of the Marquis looks taller today."

His abstraction was broken by the boy's words. He repeated to himself, "Marquis, Marquis..." And digging deep into his memory, he remembered that in the fourth year the name of the Marquis of Pombal had come up when they studied history. Continuing down the Avenue, he looked to right and left, to the right where the cars were and to the left where the trams were climbing the hill crammed with passengers. Walking and stopping and looking and making silent comments, he arrived at Restauradores. He looked at the post office. He had a sudden idea. If he sent his wife a telegram to be waiting for him at the airport on the afternoon of the 19th, maybe that was better than surprising her. Also, it had been more than thirty years. What would she be like? He went in, asked for a form and wrote:

"Maria Clara
"Achada do Castanheiro
"Boaventura, Madeira

"Arriving Madeira Saturday afternoon plane.
"Love,
"Artur."

From the post office he went along the avenue looking at what was happening around him, one step at a time, keeping a lookout when he crossed the road so as not to be run over.

In the Rossio, he thought that there were more people than anywhere else and he was amazed at the number of groups that were talking together. When he passed by the Nicola cafe, he looked in.

He saw that some of the tables were empty and remembered that he had not eaten that day. He went up to the nearest table, sat down and asked for a cup of coffee and a glass of *aguardiente*. So as not to stray from the area round his pension, he did not leave Baixa. He went along Rua do Ouro, Rua Augusta and Rua da Prata and all seemed familiar, as did Chiado. He had lunch at the Nicola. He enjoyed the afternoon. It was the shop windows that interested him most and held his gaze, almost forcing him to stop, such was the fascination that they held for him.

And many passersby, when they saw the man with the amazed expression on his face looking in the shop window, joined him, surrounded him, convinced that there was some wonderful in the shop window. They left again when they saw that there was nothing special.

In Rua do Carmo, he glanced into a shop window and his attention was caught by the display of stringed instruments. A guitar just like the one he had taken to Brazil captivated him and awakened the enthusiasm that he had had long ago when he left. Whatever it cost, he had to have it. He went into the shop. He strummed it. He liked the sound. He asked the price. Then he asked the employee to pack it as well as possible and left the shop delighted with life.

As he went down Rua do Carmo, a tall dark woman with an attractive figure walked towards him and their eyes met. He was electrified. He followed her. But the cumbersome package with the guitar prevented him from following through with his intentions.

Despite the fact that his hand was hurting from the parcel, his turmoil came from outside him, because the cause came from outside. The unknown woman looked back as she went into the Marquis Tea Room in Rua Garrett. Artur understood. He rapidly retraced his steps, turned into Rua do Carmo, went into the music shop and asked the employee to look after the guitar for him.

His desire burned like a flame, as it had when he was a youth, like the strings of a guitar producing a stronger, quivering tone. His insides were burning up and his blood was boiling with an ardour that was compelling him to feel the woman's shapely body, which reminded him of a Spanish woman. In a few moments he was back at the Marquis Tea Rooms. He found her there drinking tea. As he went up to the counter to choose a cake, he looked at her surreptitiously. And because she had already seen him, they exchanged the same penetrating looks as in the street. He paid for the cake. That *femme fatale* intuitively understood him.

Artur stood like a statue by the doorway, waiting for her. Five minutes went by that seemed endless. Suddenly, his goddess passed by, like a magical, sensual love potion. He followed her. In front of the Suiça, she caught the Campo Grande bus. Timidly, instead of sitting next to her in the vacant seat, he went to the back. He was not going to lose her. He could take a taxi back to the pension. What interested him was the adventure, reliving his first days in Brazil and Venezuela, if he reached the end, if his action had not been in vain. He did not notice when the bus stopped from time to time, as his thoughts were subordinated to his senses, watching the woman sitting there with her back to him. He did not miss the slightest movement of her head, until the bus slowed down and stopped. She stood up decidedly. They got off. The unknown woman spoke to him when she felt him almost at her side:

"You're a returnee, aren't you?"

"No, ma'am. I've just come from Venezuela."

Well, I would have sworn that I saw you here a few days ago with another man who's a relative of mine, who's just come back from Angola."

"And when I saw you, I could have sworn that you were a Spanish woman I knew in Caracas. You have her same air, the same pretty face, the same upright body…"

"Since it seems we already know each other, come to my house and we'll have a drink. I'd like to hear about your travels."

They walked to a cross street near the Avenida da República. Night was falling. A cold drizzle fell like needles on their faces. They could hear the noise of the cars rushing along. There were more cars parked by the side of the road. At the same time as Artur was having his little adventure, other men were indifferent to the suffering of their fellowmen, maybe in that street or far away, in another part of the earth, unaware of their egotism. Morality condemns them in its falsely rigid judgement of reality. The authority of reason reproves them. But what would life be without egotism? Should we censure the Venezuelan's adventure in front of his own conscience? If the force of instinct defeats the duty to be faithful, there has been a conflict. But, if there was no conflict, should we accuse the man because of his behaviour, because he was pushed by his instincts? What is the truth?

"I live here."

An old building. The stairs were not steep and so were neither irritating nor tiring. The short flights also had shallow steps.

They walked upstairs without speaking. She opened her handbag, took out a key and turned it in the lock and the door swung back on its hinges.

"Come in. It's a small house. I live alone. This is my room."

Artur sat in a armchair while she went to fetch the whisky. In a moment, she came back with a tin tray with two glasses and a bottle of Dimple. As she sipped, she told him details of her life as a widow. She had one daughter at boarding school. The difficulties were enormous. And sitting on the edge of the bed, her skirt riding up, she showed off a pair of legs that could have been sculpted by a modeller of religious statues. He was always maddened, bewitched, by the sight of legs that reminded him of Maria Clara's, and stared at them in a stupor.

"Look at that bill. I have until tomorrow to pay 1,500 escudos."

Artur felt he was being tricked but he immediately took out the money out of his wallet and gave it to her.

"Come over here, next to me."

Feeling moved and taken in by the languorous words uttered in a soft tone of voice, Artur kissed the lips that must have received thousands of kisses. His hands caressed the soft legs. Giving in to the caresses, she whispered, "Not today... It's the 18th... The day after tomorrow. It's not me who doesn't want to, it's nature."

In his disappointment, the kisses stopped tasting sweet. Why had she responded to his call to possess her? Now he never would. He was leaving next day for the Island. He would have to be his wife's for ever and this adventure would die with him, his last amorous adventure.

He did not say another word. He put on his jacket and as she went into the other room, opened the door and closed it hurriedly behind him. He went out into the night, which the street lamps were trying unsuccessfully to expel. He hailed a taxi.

"Avenida Duque de Loulé."

CHAPTER XXIV

Inês and Maria Pereira set the date for the wedding. Their children would get married in two months' time. They went to the most famous dressmaker in Caracas to order the finest dress for the bride. Carolina wanted a simple design, going against her mother's and future mother-in-law's opinion, which was to have a dress by Dior.

Fonseca Pereira ordered the reception at the hotel that was considered to be one of the best in the city, the Tamanaque.

There was still a week to go before the event when Inês received a telegram from Matilde telling her to meet her plane on Saturday at La Guaira airport. This laconic note caused delirious joy. Inês prepared a room in the house that they had recently moved into for her *comadre*. Meanwhile, Carolina and Armando invited the teachers from the university that they were on good terms with and the students with whom they were friends. The two families were living new emotions that overwhelmed the limits of the imagination but were not unknown to the human condition.

The present did not exist, or rather the present that is the linear routine of everyday life. Their consuming concern was the near future. Their *idée fixe* was the wedding, because it would perpetuate the families of Inês and Maria Pereira.

So the days flew by like a waking dream until, at ten o'clock, the plane landed and slowly crossed the runway. The passengers entered the terminal.

"Oh, Matilde!"

"Inês!"

The two old friends hugged each other tightly.

"It still seems impossible, Matilde!"

"It does to me too!"

"Carolina!"

"Godmother!" And they were reunited.

"Alfredo, look how Inês has changed!"

"Maybe! Look at all the years we haven't seen her!"

"And who would have thought that little Raquel was already a young lady!"

After collecting their luggage, Francisco Freitas went to the factory and Carolina drove their guests home.

The next night, the Fonseca Pereira family came to Inês's house to enjoy an evening with their good friends. The men talked about the places where they had been born and business. The women talked about the wedding, which would take place in two days' time, and the young people, with their usual verve, commented on everybody and everything, ironically describing the life and the preferences of the people they knew.

Matilde and Maria Pereira got on well and next day Inês and Matilde and her husband and daughter had lunch at the Fonseca Pereira's.

And they liked each other even more. In this way, a mutual respect grew up between the woman from Porto and the one from Madeira. They each found that her new friend's character was so like her own that they might have known each other since they were little girls. Inês was delighted that her best friends had become friends. She felt that they were as virtuous, spontaneous, disinterested and sincere as she was.

In this atmosphere of human warmth that makes it pleasant to be alive, the day that had so anxiously been awaited for so long arrived, a time that was subjective and personal, that only the soul sensed and was aware of.

"Carolina does look pretty, doesn't she?" said Inês to Matilde.

"That veil really suits her!" exclaimed Maria Pereira.

"She looks a picture," opined her godmother.

"My daughter!" And Carolina's mother kissed her avidly with tears in her eyes.

No one who was there would have thought that this was the simple little mountain flower with the naïve, scared eyes who had gone to the city, which she had never seen before, to her godmother's house in Crisma.

The ceremony took place in the church of Our Lady of Mercy, where the fresh voices of the Novena that was just ending could still be heard. The curious from Francisco's and Pereira's factories came to the wedding, and many acquaintances and friends of the two families.

After the ceremony, the newly weds and their guests went by car to the hotel. On a long table in the enormous dining room were bouquets of lovely, colourful flowers.

When the time came for the toast, Fonseca Pereira, visibly moved, addressed his audience, saying, "This is the happiest hour in my life since the day I got married myself. Armando, my son, has found a companion, Carolina, who brings him honour and a good name because of her womanly virtues and her intelligence. My wife and I have long thought of her as a daughter, as she is the daughter of our dearest friends, Inês and Francisco. Let's drink to the happiness of the newly weds, their parents and everyone."

That same day, Armando and Carolina left by plane to spend two weeks in Portugal. During their absence, the evenings at the Fonseca Pereira's and the Francisco Freitas' became more frequent. Matilde's husband amused himself by looking out of the factory door at the noisy, colourful movement in the street, when he was not gossiping with Francisco in his office until lunchtime and then from lunchtime till dinnertime. One evening as they were talking, Alfredo suggested that Freitas should return to the Island. They exchanged opinions.

"Francisco, I spent nearly fifteen years in Antigua and I brought back enough to be independent on nothing more than the interest that the bank gives me on the capital. It's a little fortune over there. But I understand that I ought to put part of that money into circulation so I'm thinking of setting up in business. The best thing for me would probably be a supermarket, in its own building. If I had a partner, I'd have more volume and the profits would be bigger."

"The best business, and the most profitable, can be done in a big city like this one, in a rich country. I'm doing fine, Alfredo. When the children are old enough to look after themselves, I've already thought about going back home with Inês. It's our country after all!"

"Then maybe we can get together and instead of one supermarket we can open two or three..."

"In my opinion, you have to build a big building for a big supermarket!"

"One way or another it's a big business! Funchal is a tourist town! Foodstuffs always sell... with tourism or without it. Since I came back from Antigua, as I have nothing to do, I watch what's happening in the shops. And that's why I think that a supermarket is where the capital would be safer."

And striking a match to light a cigarette, he went on, "And before other people get in on it; there's no time to be lost."

"You can start looking around for a site for sale that's not too far from the centre of the city. I'm here to share in the work. In a year or two, I'll leave Venezuela."

The conversation stopped when Jorge Ratazana came in.

"Good afternoon, Mr. Francisco. I've come to bring you some news. I saw Duarte, Cambado's son, yesterday morning. I asked him if he'd been in Venezuela long and he said he'd come on the plane last week."

"Does he have a job?"

"It seems he's looking for one."

"Listen, Jorge, if you see him or you know where he's staying, tell him to come and see me. That position that the Italian had needs to be filled."

"That would be real luck for the lad."

"He's from our part of the country. And we have to help our own first."

"That's true. But there can't be many Madeirans with a heart as open as yours."

"I forgot to ask about your wife. Is she settling in?"

"A day doesn't go by without her talking about her home in Achada."

"It's natural. As she's always alone, she has to think about something and what she remembers best are the good times when she was surrounded by the family. There's no remedy except getting used to it!"

"There are times when I lose my patience!"

"But she's right. Well. If you see Duarte, or he comes knocking on your door, send him to see me."

Francisco Freitas's kind heart was shown in these gestures, which came from a nature that was inclined to do good, just as the eyes of an artist are born for beauty, and with them he looked at the world, the other nature, the exterior one, the one that exists in physical space and is full of inarticulate life, from the smallest plant that feeds animal life to the leafy, evergreen tree that does not understand but also fights for life, an anonymous fight, that cannot be expressed visibly: he saw the little trees that wanted to grow but were stunted by the bigger, arrogant trees standing next to them. This daily, unconscious observation was part of his emotional make-up. Saddened, he never forgot the explanation of Mr. Vigario and his teacher, Jorge, that vegetation also formed a world like that of Man. But only people who think can do good, not trees, which are alive because they are born and grow and can lose their lives at the hands of Man or simply because they are mortal.

He did not think that he had come into the world to do good, although this was how he behaved to his fellow countrymen. Doing good was not an idea that lit up his mind; it was what he was. And if being generous to Ratazana and Duarte was goodness, it was because the situation provided the opportunity. Although there could be goodness in him, he had never noticed that he had it. And his goodness was only seen in actions. Now, thinking back, he realised why he had this feeling. Jorge had confirmed it, by saying that his heart was open to the unfortunate.

Francisco Freitas felt that his philanthropic gestures, his charitable attitude to Ratazana and Duarte, were a love that was bound to the cottage, the fruition of a time when a boy's bare feet trod the earth that had turned to mud in the January rain. In them, in their faces and their speech, he saw a well loved vision of the poor folk, the square with the fire game, and the mountains, the mountains where the night dwells and witches have their hidey-holes. In them, just like the bowed vines reflected in the river, the photograph of Freitas' distant past was never erased. Rather, it was enlivened, without embarrassment, by a feeling of hurtful

humiliation. He enjoyed the contrast of what he had been with what he had now, in terms of wealth and a place in society.

Putting aside these sentimental memories, their evocative power was replaced by the reasoning of an immigrant who has triumphed over the hard life of a slave.

Being an immigrant, when you cannot get away from the boss's nagging or of the misery of poverty by becoming financially independent, is to be the plaything of fate and the plagues that visit you. A foreign land is a stepmother that cannot feel pain. So, you have to go on rotting on your own strip of land or under the yoke of a fellow man, with no ambition to cause you anguish, offend your reason or inflame your imagination.

He was saddened to see many of his compatriots earning a weekly or monthly wage and then spending it all and sleeping at night on park benches like tramps. They were not interested in tomorrow, only today and the indulgent pleasures of earthly life.

That night, after spending the evening at the Fonseca Pereira's, Francisco talked to his wife when they were in their room together.

"When we were talking at the office, Alfredo tried to convince me that if we opened a big supermarket in Funchal, the two of us, we could live at home and I could build up the fortune I've made in Venezuela."

"Look, Francisco, that's not a bad idea. We've been here for fifteen years. Carolina has married well and she'll certainly make her life here. Armando has to supervise his father's factory. Anabela would come with us and, as she's a doctor, her living is guaranteed. And Carlos should marry the daughter of that industrialist who's a friend of Mr. Fonseca Pereira and with his legal studies he'll become his father-in-law's lawyer."

"Even if António hadn't come along to spur my enthusiasm for opening a business, there was already something inside of me that was attracted by the idea of going home. We could have a quiet life! And to do that, there's nowhere in the world that's better than the place where you were born."

Inês, who was very happy with her husband's way of thinking, thought about living in the city in a modern building, going out in her car, having the best connections, going with Matilde to sophisticated events, to big hotels, going to mass at the Cathedral in dresses from the most famous couturiers. Just thinking that this future was realizable made her feel a new woman and young again.

After all, she was the mother of a foreign trained woman doctor and the newspapers would have to put that in the news.

"You're right, Francisco. If everything goes right and we leave Venezuela, we'll go back to the land where we were born. We can be part of the best society. We're rich; our children have university degrees. We'll be invited to all those famous parties with the best families."

"Inês, we've always been happy. We always agree with each other. What you like, I like too. I owe you a lot because you have, and always have had, good ideas and a good head on your shoulders."

And in the silence of the night, the big clock in the drawing room struck four, and the chimes could be heard through the bedroom door.

CHAPTER XXV

It was six o'clock in the evening. Night was falling. The *Sacadura Cabral*, which had had come from Belgium, landing just before six, began to slowly taxi down the runway, bound for Funchal. Artur was about to miss that plane, as he had the one at four o'clock. He had gone that morning to visit Sintra, which he had so much wanted to see since he had heard some Portuguese from Lisbon, who were fanatical about its beauty, gossiping about it. The train that took him to old Sintra arrived at the station at ten o'clock. He climbed up a steep path to the castle on the rocks. He looked at the battlements and did not know what they for. He was not scared by the twisted trees because he had braved the ti plants and ironwood trees on the mountains of Boaventura. He felt hungry after the tiring walk. When he got back to the town, he had lunch in a restaurant that opened out onto a square that was swept by a chilly breeze. He got back to Lisbon well after two o'clock. His adventure was still on his mind, although he felt sorry for his wife after the confession that he had made.

The crowded, heavy aircraft climbed to over a thousand metres. They began to feel some turbulence and they had to keep their seatbelts fastened. Because he had been the last passenger on board, the Venezuelan had not stowed his guitar and had it on his lap. He was worried by the stormy journey. Time passed by. The hostess announced that the plane was coming down to the city and that they should keep their seatbelts fastened as they were being constantly buffeted by the wind that dark night, as the unrelenting rain fell like stair rods. The plane came to the runway. The pilot tried to land but after two failed attempts he gained height. The wind lessened but the intermittent rain was like smoke. On the terrace of the terminal, all those who were expecting friends or family crowded together under umbrellas. Suddenly, the plane hit the runway by the airport road and rolled out of control onto the rocks. A loud bang was heard in the blackness of the night. Flames poured out of the plane, which broke up into three parts.

The crowd of waiting people that had seen the scene unfold in seconds began to scream and to jump down to the wreckage and the wounded and dead.

Groans were heard from the fire that engulfed the plane. But who could go in without being killed! Wildly, faced with the horrific scene and the sounds of death rattles and suffering, Clara went up to a middle-aged man who was lying on the seashore. Would it be Artur? How would she recognise him after thirty-five years? Would his features have changed? Bewildered, her cries were added to those of the people around her, "Oh, Artur, my Artur!'

Next to the wreckage of the aeroplane, lit by a circle of light was a head without a body. She scoured the scene of the tragedy with a man who had a bulls-eye lantern and was looking for his wife.

"Oh, sir, did no one else escape?"

"It seems not. More than a hundred people died."

"My husband was in there!" Oh Lord! My Artur was in there!"

And all night they took the burned bodies to the hospital.

This is man's destiny on earth, as he lived, so he dies. Man does not look for death: fate sets up traps using the hands of other men. That is what happened to Icarus, the legendary fugitive from the labyrinth, with his waxen wings.

Clara went to the hospital. She asked about her husband but a nurse said that he must have disappeared into the sea or been burned alive. On the Sunday, she took the bus to Boaventura and thought the trip was longer than on other days. In Igreja, where she got off, she walked slowly, thinking over the worst thing that had happened to her, the death of Artur. She forgot his ingratitude and his lack of judgement where women were concerned, which had made him not send her any news or answer her letters for more than thirty years.

When she lifted her eyes up from the ground, she saw Pinga's house. On the road outside the neighbours were raising their arms and chattering.

Joana from Moinho cried out, "How awful! More than a hundred people were killed!"

"How did the plane crash?" asked Gerardo's daughter.

"Who knows! Only God knows," said Virginia.

"Look! Here comes Clara, who went to wait for her husband," exclaimed Joana.

And in a moment they all went to meet her as they heard her exclaiming, "Oh, my husband! Poor me!" and crying and sobbing.

"But what happened? Tell us!" insisted Joana.

Clara sat down on the stone wall that faced the street and told them about the weather and the plane sliding off the runway. How afterwards it broke into three parts and how the fire had killed most of the people and then she told them about the people who had been swallowed up by the sea and then, opening up her heart, she said,

"The lucky ones are those who were saved and are recovering in hospital."

But the memory of Artur rose in her mind and a sudden sob made her voice break.

"Patience, Clara! Don't think about it. He was a terrible ingrate. It's been more than thirty years since he wanted to hear about you!" said Virginia.

And the others agreed with her, "It's true."

That Sunday, Achada was a livid colour. It was one of those strange evenings that turn to a silent night broken only by the lowing of a cow in a barn, tied to the manger, waiting for its bundle of grass. The water was flowing in the ravine. The breeze that was blowing down from the mountain smelt of winter and of rain washed leaves.

CHAPTER XXVI

After staying for eighteen days at Inês's house, Alfredo's family left by plane for the Island. The separation was the cause of painful thoughts. The feelings of mutual affection that linked them all had grown stronger, with the strength of things that time will only unravel in the unforeseeable future. Sighing, Inês promised her friend Matilde that it would not be many years before they saw each other again and then they would be together for the rest of their lives.

And so they met eagerly, either at Fonseca Perreira's or at Inês's house. Since she had become a close friend of Maria, Inês had learned her ways of receiving company, of doing people favours, of expressing herself with just the right words and the correct adjectives, and had corrected her way of pronouncing words. None of the rules of society escaped her and, indeed, she cultivated the taste that characterizes ladies. Also, since she had heard her children studying every day, her head was slowly filled with knowledge that she knew how to use with prudence and in the right circumstances, as she had the critical sense of an intelligent woman who was always sensible. She was the confidante of Mrs. Maria Pereira, who listened to her opinion on the simplest things and then adopted them, as her friend's astute thoughts on certain details uncovered what had been hidden from her before: women's fashion, organizing a wardrobe or the place to hang a picture, here or over there, instead of a piece of furniture that was moved somewhere else. Inês hurried over when her best friend phoned, ready to do whatever was needed.

On one occasion, after returning from shopping, when the two women thought they were alone, Inês revealed her husband's idea of returning home sometime in the near future. Maria Pereira felt the suffering that would come some day and could not accept it. She tried to convince Inês to make long visits to Madeira every year, rather than a definitive move, because her husband's financial situation was also based on deeper and deeper foundations every year. Inês was moved.

"I'll talk to Francisco. Our friendship is eternal, in this world. Our children have already united us even further."

"You know very well that you're like a sister to me."

"I know! I know! I feel a sincere friendship for you, and yours for me is part of my life."

***

The correspondence between Alfredo and Freitas became almost monthly. Alfredo's latest letter had said:

"I'm almost ready to make a deal to buy an old building near St. Paul's. My idea is to have the houses demolished and build a big building for both a house and a shop. It will be the biggest supermarket in the city."

Francisco Freitas rejoiced over the words. However, thinking about what Inês had told him about her conversation with Carolina's mother-in-law, he was filled with sadness.

After rereading the long sheet of paper, he folded it up, went to his wife, read the letter again and said to her,

"What if I show this to Fonseca Pereira? He knows about our business and we owe the good fortune God has given us to him."

"I was just going to tell you to do that. Show him the letter, although the idea of the business may hurt him. Don't take any decision without listening to him."

"It's a difficult one. At the same time, I'd love to go back home."

"What if you become Alfredo's partner and you go back there for the first few years, just for the year end balance?"

"I'm going to see Fonseca Pereira today."

And, changing the subject, while her husband was putting the letter into his jacket pocket, she said, "I have some great news! I think that Carolina is going to have a baby."

"We're going to have a Venezuelan grandchild?"

"That's how life is. He won't be a Madeiran like us."

"But one day he has to see Achada, where we were born!"

And Francisco got into his car to go to Fonseca Pereira's factory. He found him in his office bending over a graph of the week's production.

"How is my friend Freitas?"

"Same as usual."

"Good."

Without continuing the usual pleasantries, Freitas took the letter out of the envelope, opened it and exclaimed,

"Please read this, my friend."

Fonseca Pereira turned the paper over and over again. And because his normal reasoning was for the material problems of business and this had diluted his emotions even for his friends, he opined,

"I think you should accept! It will be a source of great profits. Don't think twice!"

"But how can I be here and there?"

"In my opinion, you should try. If you intend to return home, either you sell the factory or you set up a company with no more than two people that you can trust."

"I'm going to take your advice. And since this is only a plan, there's time to think about it."

CHAPTER XXVII

Gregório was getting used to the work schedule at Mr. Daniel's factory. He did not have to worry about doing the accounts after buying and selling cattle. He changed his rustic habits as he got used to living in the city with two comrades from the North of Portugal. One had emigrated from the outskirts of Viana do Castelo and the other had come from way out in Barroso. When they left the factory, they went to the beer bar and spend part of the evening drinking, gossiping and telling picaresque stories that caused great laughter. One night, some tough looking individuals came up and asked them where they were from. Gregório was not bothered and told them who he was, but the one from Viana replied, "I don't have to give any satisfaction to people I don't know." And he continued talking to his companions.

The most daring of the newcomers raised his arm aggressively but the man from Viana immediately hit him so hard on the back of the neck that he fell down on the floor. It was like a match to a fuse. In a moment, the others, who had seen what happened, jumped on the three of them from all sides and during this interval Gregório grabbed a jug of water and threw it into the face of one of the rowdies. And the fight started again, ending when the lights in the room were turned out. Then the groups broke up, although the calmest of the bunch, who had kept out of it, had his nose bloodied by an unseen opponent.

Gregório partied like this every night with one of the merrymakers who slept outside on a park bench. Lunch was almost always his main meal. For dinner, he had a beer and a sandwich.

Wouldn't the simple life that he had led before he started to swill beer in the city make one more aware of the struggle to earn one's bread and therefore more insistent on looking into the future and dreaming constantly of providing for it?

Gregório forgot the habits that were good for his health and for his finances and acquired some that were bad both for his health and for his savings. This life, lived only in the present, was driving him crazy: he went on earning and wasting his money. It was not like being in the village, where life started a little after dawn when the shadows that came down from the sky did not make the shapes stand out.

Bajeca's son made excuses to himself when he had no money, comparing his life with that of other immigrants, his peers, which was just the same as his. In the evenings, when he heard his group of friends make references to rich immigrants, he fell silent and, without hating himself, the thought came to him of rebelling against his lack of willpower and overcoming the most difficult obstacles that many, who came from the far end of other parishes that bordered on his, had triumphed over. He did not envy them. But what good did it do his conscience to criticize behaviour that he did not have? He was sorry for his father's past and he could not run away from his heritage. And he thought to himself that what other people had inherited was the strength to overcome their will.

In this way, living from one day to the next, he was not making anyone unhappy. He was a bachelor and he stayed that way, for good or for ill. But suddenly, he remembered that this was not quite true. His mother was sorry for his wrongheadedness. At least he had that! In the last letter that she had written to him, she had said:

"Son, be sensible. You're young now and have your health but tomorrow you'll be old and weak."

Emigrating, leaving his homeland, had not been good for him. Oh no! What if he changed? But who could run away from his heritage?

Gregório wanted to express the ideas that bubbled inside him like boiling water, but he did not have the words to express them properly.

CHAPTER XXVIII

When the plane hit the ground, the impact somehow shot Artur out with his guitar still in his hands; he had no idea how. He stumbled away and some firemen found him as night was turning into day. They were going to take him to the hospital but confusion reigned at the edge of the field. At the entrance, the vehicles were blocking each other's way and they were trying to get the badly injured away from that madhouse, so, when two of the firemen went to help an ambulance that was calling for them, Artur, although he was half stunned, got out of the vehicle and went straight to Santo António. He knew the path like the palm of his hand as it climbed up to Estrela. It was flat for most of the way through the pine trees with their green needles and then dipped down to where Curral could be seen. Then the narrow path snaked along and in the end came out on the level ground where the houses and the church were evidence of human habitation.

The sky cleared. After getting the numbness out of his legs, a desire to see his wife, the house and his children strengthened his muscles. The pine trees made the path dark. The wind dropped. Artur passed his hand over his face and felt that he had been hurt. He could not explain how he had scratched his face nor how he had escaped the infernal fire. His legs hurt. He made a walking stick out of a branch that he found, which made him feel better as it eased the tightness in his leg muscles. He did not go down the dangerous bends on the edge of the precipice; he did not dream of doing that. He felt more confident on the new road. He groped his way across the potholes and, cautiously, afraid of falling, came to a clearing. He asked himself how many hours he had walked that day. His mind knew he had walked a long way but not his watch, which, as it did not have luminous hands, was worthless. He saw a light under a door. He knocked. Opening the half door, the shopkeeper looked out horrified at Artur and asked,

"Whatever happened to you? Your suit's all singed and there's blood in your hair. What happened?"

Artur told him about the tragedy of the plane and his odyssey that night. He asked them to let him rest in a corner of the shop and there he slept. About midday he woke up hungry. He had some money so he bought some bread and a tin of tuna.

"Have some cherry brandy to warm up and put some strength in those legs now that you're going to go over the mountain."

"How much is it?"

"You don't have to pay anything. It's a gift!"

He thanked the man and set off on trembling legs, leaning on a walking staff that the shopkeeper had lent him.

He climbed up the rough path that was made difficult by the branches of the trees that covered it and made it dark. He preferred the wide stretches but the thick, interlocking branches made him stop frequently, as well as the fact that his legs were not obeying him.

Around five o'clock he was just about to come out in Lombo do Urzal. He felt exhausted and that his bones were broken. When he looked out over the broad valley between the proud mountains, he stood still and said to himself, "My village! It's been thirty-five years since I left you. I was young then. Now..." And he started to make his way down, wrapped in the fog that had built up behind the mountains tops, slipping and sliding...

Night caught him there. The bridge over the Porco was left behind. At the end of the road, next to the church, he could see the figures of two boys. He turned onto the road to Achada do Castanheiro. He was amazed that the road was tarmacced. There, he heard the water falling on the stones in the river. As he got nearer to the house, he became nervous. There was no one there. He came nearer and nearer... He heard weeping and cries and frantic expressions: "Oh, my Artur! I'd forgive him for everything!" And then convulsive sobbing. He pushed the door open. He went in. Alda, his married daughter, with tears in her eyes, did not recognize him but did not have time to ask the stranger what he wanted.

When he saw the woman sitting on the old pine bench, clutching her head in her hands, he put down the guitar on the table and ran to her, put his arms round her and said, "Clara! Clara!"

The unlikely event made her faint, because it was so unbelievable. And she remained unconscious for some seconds.

"You're burnt, neighbour!" exclaimed Virginia.

"But he got here alive," said Pestana's Leonilde, pulling on the arm of the little one who was putting his hand into a chipped clay bowl half full of wheat.

This was how Artur returned, with his memory full of experiences that he had known and seen in far off lands but with no money for a peaceful old age in the land of his birth. He had emigrated when he was a young man, before his sun had reached its zenith. Maria Clara, a slim girl, full of life, had stayed behind with their last child still in her belly. She had radiated youth, vigour and freshness, in the agility of her body, in the pink skin of her face and her sparkling mischievous eyes.

Now, thirty-five years later, worn down by care, she was older than her husband. She stooped slightly: her hair was the colour of flax; her skin was wrinkled by the weather and a waxen colour, except for her prominent cheekbones that had turned purple, where once it had been as smooth as that of a saint sculpted by the inspired hands of a ceramist. And to change her even more, some spectacles with cheap frames perched on the end of her nose, robbing her of her identity as Maria Clara from Achada.

For thirty-five years, Maria Clara had suffered the lacerating pain of being abandoned by her husband. For part of that time, she had lived a bitter life. Two little strips of land hardly produced enough to feed them: some potatoes in spring, some beans in June and some pumpkins and pimpernels. If she had not embroidered from daybreak till the dead of night, how could she have raised her children!

Whenever she had remembered Artur, she had cried aloud bitterly, "Artur! To me, that ne'er do well is dead!"

Artur returned, worn out, disillusioned, to find shelter in his wife's thatched cottage. The two scanty strips of land that Maria Clara had inherited had never increased. Brazil and Venezuela had lighted up his senses. He had been fascinated by a present that had also hidden his future. But his life had been saved, with half a dozen thousand escudo notes in his pocket and his guitar, the symbol of his fate. And so he readapted to his old habits and to being a cobbler, sitting on the same three-legged stool as before, when he worked in his old shop with the green painted chestnut wood door, which squatted on the old road where the houses turn their backs on the churchyard. He was not leaving there again. He built a shed on the little square for a cobbler's shop to welcome his customers.

Those who had known him in Juiz de Fora and Caracas would never have recognised Artur, wandering around in his pyjamas, as the man who had fallen in love with the woman from Baía and was the idol of the Spanish woman. He had come back in two ways: in space, to Achada, and in time, regressing to a childhood that old age unconsciously celebrates, one that is rooted in the earth and in people. The old man was living as if he had not yet emigrated.

CHAPTER XXIX

The plot in São Paulo, near Carreira St., cost 2.600.000 escudos. It was bought by Alfredo de Sousa and Francisco Freitas. It did not take the workers long to demolish the old house, which had been built at the beginning of the nineteenth century, and to level out the land, making the street look less crowded and the buildings on the opposite side of the street less closed in.

Spring was coming to an end when the trenches for the foundations of the new building were dug. The walls began to rise soon after and the work went on without pause until they had gained their full height.

In Caracas, Francisco Freitas was living through days of agonised confusion. He had to decide what to do about the factory: whether to sell it or to keep it and take on people he knew and trusted who would give him guarantees of their character, honesty and diligence.

He talked it over with Inês, who was aware of his dilemma, and her opinion prevailed: the best course was to take on two partners. Freitas then started to take mental stock of all his employees, from the ones with the most seniority to those who had recently been hired. After spending hours at his desk thinking and making his choice, he decided on his fellow countrymen, who had never been far from his thoughts when the idea of a partnership came up. He also looked at the list of the other workers, because it was a good idea to know who would be working for them.

One afternoon, when he got home, Inês asked, "So, you've chosen your partners?"

"I'd already found them before I decided to go into business with Alfredo."

"Who are they?"

"Ratazana and Duarte, Cambado's son."

"Then I have to say you made a good choice."

"They're people from our parish, but that's not the only reason. There is a good reason why Ratazana should be my partner. Do you remember that strike that the workers were going to have and that didn't happen? If it hadn't been for Ratazana, they would have gone on strike. He was my secret agent. I owe him for that. Almost every afternoon he came to my office and told me all that he'd seen and heard. And Duarte, Cambado's son, is a serious person and he works well, according to what Ratazana says."

"Look, Francisco, with those partners we can rest easy."

"I'd already thought of them, although I did look at everybody."

At dinner, seated around the table, Anabela asked her father when he was going to the Island and he replied that it would be very soon.

"Do I have to practise medicine?"

"I think so. That's why you took that degree," said her mother.

"It seems to me that we are rich enough for me to be able not to have a consulting room."

"Good fortune belongs to God, my girl!"

"There you go with your homilies!"

"No. It's good for you to remember that if today we have something, tomorrow we could have nothing. Everything is possible in this world."

"Anabela, mother is right," said Carlos.

Anabela fell silent and kept her eyes on her plate, with an air of being quiet because she had been defeated, and she did not say another word until the meal was over.

Anabela had a touchy character; so much so that Inês confessed to Maria Pereira one night at a party at her house, that the doctor was very dictatorial.

On Saturday, before lunch, Francisco Freitas sent for Ratazana and Duarte to come to his office and told them of his intentions. They looked at each as much in joy as surprise. In their emotion, they were at a loss for words.

"Mr. Francisco, we were born in Achada. We all belong to the same family. You can count on our loyalty," exclaimed Ratazana.

"I believe you because I know you. Next week we'll sign the papers for the partnership for the factory."

That evening, the two families met at Inês's house. Fonseca Pereira was delighted with the news that Freitas gave him and the partners that he had chosen. That way, the factory would thrive. The profits were increasing and were assured. He had met Ratazana and Duarte once when he went to the office and the few words that they had exchanged had impressed him as he thought that they would not cheat and that their faces reflected their feelings.

Mrs. Maria could not resign herself to her friend and family leaving, especially Inês, her sister, as she kindly called her. But because dispersion is a law of life, which explained why the Fonseca Pereira family was in Venezuela, Mrs. Maria thought about the phenomenon of being and not being, and staying and not staying, which shares something with being. And if suffering is also part of life, there is no remedy except to accept Man's destiny passively, as change is a part of his existence. And to soothe the inevitable, the two couples promised to do something that would not be hard to do in the long run: not to spend all their time in Venezuela nor in Madeira.

Carlos would stay on at his parent's house as he was a bachelor, and after getting married, he would preside over the meetings of the partners in the bakery, although he was already busy taking care of the his future father-in-law's business. Time did not stand still and neither did life, since it exists because of time and cannot abandon it.

Inês was missing her family, Matilde and her homeland.

***

When the plane landed on the 'Santa Catarina' runway, there was a blood red sunset and the breeze that was blowing down from the Santo mountains brought the freshness of the heights with it. Matilde, her husband and daughter were waiting impatiently for their friends and as soon as they came out of the luggage claim, after their suitcases had been inspected by customs, they hugged them in long embraces with much heartfelt nostalgia.

"It's still seems impossible," said Inês in an emotional tone of voice.

"To me too," said Matilde, hugging Anabela.

"Let's go," exclaimed Alfredo to Francisco Freitas.

"Will we all fit in?" he asked.

"If we squash up. It's a big car," replied Raquel.

And so Alfredo started the car. In Pináculo, they stopped to see the enticing view of the city.

Inês's gaze wandered beyond the last little stars on the hill, on the road to the north. Thoughts of her parents, the modest home in which she had been born and her own humble cottage distracted her.

Her family's past, her past as a girl and the land, the land, that little place in between the mountains excited her imagination. It had grown green in her memory just as a place becomes green again in the spring breeze, with the strength of a feeling that had been held captive by the remote past. When she was far away, the distance was great and it stopped being a place in three dimensions and lost its depth, to become a presence, a sensation, life. Her thoughts were overwhelmed by a desire to see the object of these feelings with her own eyes and so her eyes moved to the road to the north and her thoughts raced off into the distance.

***

December. The air was soft with an autumnal warmth and the sky was stormy, when it was not turquoise blue. The house in Avenida do Infante, where Francisco Freitas, Inês and Anabela would live, was surrounded by a veranda with capricious balustrades, from which one's eyes could see the beauty of the green tops of the trees, the Japanese cedars, acacias, cedars, eucalyptus and jacarandas and fall in love with the flowers in the garden. A profusion of small plants lay humbly waiting for the spring to come and make the souls of these perennial flowers arrogant, like the gerbera daisies, which are not always the same.

The car stopped at the Avenida do Infante outside the iron gate. Alfredo opened the gate with a quick turn of the key. And in seconds they were all treading on the fitted carpet of the ground floor corridor.

Inês and Anabela both liked the house; Matilde had had Casa Cayres decorate and furnish it in the English style. In the dining room were an inlaid sideboard, a dining table with a pedestal and metal claw feet, cane bottomed chairs, a card table and a china cabinet with twelve panes of glass. In the spacious bedrooms were traditional Madeiran beds, a mahogany wardrobe, a chest of drawers, a dressing table, an old Brazilian mahogany trunk and bedside tables with marble tops. The drawing room and other rooms had sofas and armchairs, a bureau with shelves, a card table, crystal chandeliers hanging from the ceiling, sofa tables with painted candlesticks, Persian rugs, shantung curtains and a round table covered with a plush cloth.

***

Next day, Inês spent two hours in a place that she had been far away from for many years: Achada do Castanheiro.

The trip brought her both happiness and dissatisfaction. But the dissatisfaction filled her mother's heart with pain: Anabela regretted not having stayed in the city and having left the city limits.

She thought the place was very rustic and the people uncivilised.

"I didn't need to meet your parents," she said to her mother.

"But they are your grandparents, my girl!"

"I know that, but I didn't have to meet them!"

"Look here, your grandmother used to put you on her lap!"

"Yes, maybe. I don't remember that, and that's good."

Inês was struck still and felt wounded in her very soul. She did not want to tell her husband about the short conversation with her daughter so that he did not get angry.

An indescribable anguish seized her mother's heart after lunch. Inês, her husband and Anabela had enjoyed the meal very much, and Anabela praised the chicken and potatoes for having a flavour she had never tasted before.

But an intolerable anguish wrung her heart when Anabela thoughtlessly said to her grandmother, "With your hair like that you look like a witch. Don't you go to the city to have it done?"

Anabela should have been reasonable. Country folk, who live by tilling the earth, don't worry about getting their hair done. Inês scolded her for her thoughtlessness, making her see that if she had not emigrated her life would have been like her grandmother's.

To this she replied, "If I hadn't left here, I would still have made myself different from these people, all by myself!"

CHAPTER XXX

In his parents' deserted house, Carlos observed the contrast between life and death, between the sound of voices and laughter and the absence of the people who were the laughter and the voices. He felt that a void had opened up in his life, far from the warmth of his parents after they left for the Island. He felt all this because he was an introvert. He had adored his mother when he was a child, running around with a hoop outside the house in Achada and obeying her warnings when she scolded him and then kissed him tenderly with a sudden impulsive sweetness. He did not forget those memories of a childhood that was set in time, in the time he knew still lived inside him, because he had kept mental photographs of the innocent scenes of life in the rustic surroundings in which he had been born and where he had learned to love the simplicity of his parents' way of life, all that he remembered of the distant past, as intangible pictures that had never been erased.

He had trained as an engineer. For four years he had been dating another university student, Paquita, who was from Caracas. A tall, rather dark girl, she was the daughter of a Venezuelan industrialist. Her father was in favour of her marrying the foreigner, because he was the son of a humble immigrant. He recognised his intelligence and his strong, untiring, manly character. Carlos was just the man to work with him as the administrator of his factories.

After his parents left, not a week went by without Carlos meeting Ratazana, sometimes in the office and sometimes at Ratazana's house. One evening at dusk, that noisy hour when the shops close, Carlos knocked on the door.

"Ah, it's the engineer! My husband hasn't come home yet. Please come in."

Carlos waited in the little living room while Rosa unburdened herself of how much she missed her poor house in Achada. She was always sorry that she had left what was most dear to her. Then she thought of the two sheep that her father had given her to feed every morning. Carlos listened to her, and after hearing it so often, despite his education, her complaints brought back memories of his own childhood. And without knowing why he thought of *A Consolation for the Tribulations of Israel:*

> '*As dawn broke, before the serene Eastern sky was stained blood-red, they left with their flocks; and with a slow step they trod the dewy grass, listening to the sweet songs of the birds that peacefully and protectively led them to some fresh, delicious meadow;...*'

He understood that Ratazana's wife had brought with her from Achada, in her spirit and her memories, the most important part of her life, her childhood and adolescence. She had never had any ambition. And because of this, there she was in a land that was not hers and which she could not get used to. She told him that at night she woke up wanting to go back to her dream because in it she could sense her mother stroking the sheep that followed her like a puppy, stopping when she did and trailing along behind when she moved on.

Carlos was silent, as if he had been turned to stone, as he felt Rosa's words echo in his memory, the memory of a rock on the mountain in Achada echoing to the shouts of the boys, for whom the real world was limited to the area in which they ran around from sunrise to sunset. He looked at her. He was struck by her tightened face, her puckered mouth, with lips that held back silent questions and her glazed eyes that stared at him but did not see him because her thoughts were in Achada.

Carlos had found a second home in Venezuela. He had studied there and was marrying into wealth. But, despite having a personality with Venezuelan spirits, due to having studied at the university, lived with his fellow students and read local writers, his family heritage, the voice of the blood, still survived in his reactions when someone talked of his homeland and his humble relatives. It had remained with him from the early days of his childhood, living in the wild roughness of that thorny, craggy place and in the language of its people, with its phonetic phenomena, such as pronouncing "week" like "wake" and "clean" like "lane", and where the language is all about concrete things and the nouns that denote everyday things. A dormant affection for what lay far away had grown, deep in Carlos' soul, after he had been subjected to a change of country, habits, social milieu and spiritual growth. That was why he understood Rosa's fondness for Achada.

"You know, my husband is quite the opposite. This is his home. He feels as at ease here as if he'd been born here. He doesn't want anyone to talk about Achada, where he lived a life of misery. The same things goes for Duarte's Lucinda: she says they shouldn't talk about going back there. You know, sir, it's true that we don't want for anything. We have plenty of food, clothes and good shoes. I don't know why I feel as if something is missing and I don't know what it is."

"So you don't like a pretty city like this one, Rosa? The houses, the streets, the cars going around…"

"It's so noisy all day that it gives me a headache!"

They heard a door close. And then,

"Good day, Engineer."

It was Ratazana. His face glowed with happiness. His beard was closely trimmed and he was wearing a blue suit with neatly creased trousers.

"So the bakery's already too small for this parish! It's a good sign."

"Last month's income was double that of any previous month. You'll be able to see it in writing at the next meeting."

"So you're not sorry you came…"

"Not at all! This is a great country. And if I'm doing well, I owe it all to your dad. You know that! I'm going to become a Venezuelan citizen. It's necessary to take advantage of politics when it's in our interests. It's always one vote more."

"My father wrote to me a few days ago and as well as a lot of questions he asked one about you. Do you love Venezuela as much as Achada?"

"Your dad asked me that same question a long time ago and as I didn't answer it because I was thinking about the bakery, now he's asking you. Mr. Francisco must be aware that this is my country.

And the best proof is my becoming a citizen. Our business is one of those that has a future that will never die. And as to Duarte, let's not even mention him. His wife, Lucinda, says that Mr. Francisco is his second father. She has a framed picture of him in the living room. And she's right. Your father was the one who made us Venezuelans."

"Your wife is the one who can't get used to being here."

"It seems to me that having emigrated was like an illness for Rosa."

"She's missing home."

Meanwhile Carlos automatically stretched out his left arm to see his watch under his sleeve: it was twelve o'clock.

***

After his parents went back to the Island, Carlos ate at his fiancée's house, while he was a bachelor and also when he was married. His own home was only a place to spend the night. His father-in-law, Ramon, gave his son-in-law the responsibility of administering the oil refineries. As he was astute, active and entrepreneurial, Carlos dedicated himself to making even more profit from selling fuel oils. His father-in-law was delighted. He thought that Paquita's marriage to the immigrant was divine grace. While other foreigners were thinking about making their fortunes to enrich their own countries, Carlos behaved like a good Venezuelan: he increased his father-in-law's capital, with the aim that he had told him about: to become an industrialist like his father-in-law. But Carlos, the engineer, who spoke Spanish as if it had been his language from the cradle, spoke Portuguese at all the meetings and with his family. Fortunately, when people did not understand him, he then explained his ideas in a correct phrase in good Spanish, analysing them, and then went back to Portuguese, proud to speak the language he had learned as a child in his real homeland.

CHAPTER XXXI

The months went by. The profits of the business in Caracas grew. Ratazana and Duarte tried to get the maximum return from the bakery by extending the counter and putting in a new cash register. Everything went well for everyone and Francisco Freitas and Ratazana maintained a steady correspondence. In the last letter in November, his partner in Venezuela told Francisco that the Fonseca Pereira family was going to surprise them by appearing in Madeira in December. It was a secret and so he should keep the news to himself and not tell his wife.

In the midst of all this, Gregório, Bajeca's son, left Daniel's factory and, disappointed by the fact that he no longer had the bolivars to spend on gambling and beer, he asked two companions from his evenings out for a loan, got a month's advance on his wages from his boss and tried to buy a plane ticket. When he got to the travel agency, after waiting for half an hour, he put his hand in his jacket pocket and could not find his passport. He was sure that he had brought it with him. He put his hand in his pocket again and his fingers went through a hole into the lining. That was where the passport went, he thought, hurriedly, but that's not possible, even if it fell through the hole, it would still be inside the lining. And so he went back to his room determinedly. He opened his suitcase and found the passport. Delighted, he started to run, panting back to the travel agency, which closed at noon. When he had the ticket, he already felt he was on his way, but a mortifying idea came to him: he didn't have a present to take back for his mother and his money was running out. Thoughtfully, he went down the street. So many years here and there, earning and spending money and now, when he went home, his mother would ask him if he had had the good sense to save money, and he couldn't lie. He remembered his neighbour Gaspar, who was so rich he had bought three buildings in the city as an investment and gone back to live in the village. But he was consoled by another thought: his father had emigrated too and gone back home empty-handed. His luck had been like his father's, except that his underhandedness in business had not been as brazen as his father's. The thought that had not quite gone away came back to him again and repeated itself: something for his mother.

So absorbed was he, he did not notice the movement around him. Suddenly, without knowing why, he remembered a statue of a saint, the patron saint of the village, to whom he had paid his respects when he was a child by putting flowers on the pedestal by the saint's feet, together with a group of village girls of his own age. He had certainly lost his faith due to the misfortunes of his life but the idea of taking his mother a medallion filled him with happiness. He saw a little medallion in a shop that looked like the one his father had given him for his communion. He asked the price, took two bolivars out of his purse and asked the assistant to put it in a little cardboard box.

He packed the fibre suitcase that he had been lent at one time by Dionísio from Falca, his host when he lived near São Paulo and was working on a coffee plantation. His only personal belongings were five shirts, two of which were worn around the collar, a pair of trousers, a jacket and a pair of down-at-heel shoes. He also had some socks, handkerchiefs and some underpants with holes in them.

And so he said farewell to Venezuela, the land of his perdition.

***

When he arrived at the village, he went up the lane. In front of the house, his father, wearing ragged trousers, was watering the butter beans. His mother was scaring off the woodpeckers that were getting into the kitchen, which was filled with smoke from the pinecones burning on the hearth.

"My son!" She hugged him to her breast.

Gregório Bajeca exclaimed with tears in his eyes,

"After so many years, mother, the fortune I earned was to come back home. Believe me, I never forgot you!"

And taking the cardboard box out of his suitcase, he took out the medallion and said, "Here, mother!"

***

It was a peaceful morning in December when the Fonseca Pereira family got off the plane in Santa Catarina.

"What a delightful temperature!"

Maria Pereira looked around and was fascinated by the geography of the surrounding area. However, one thought remained stubbornly in her mind, her friend Inês. She wanted to see her, to exchange impressions with her, to be near the woman who was like her sister, as if the same family blood ran in her veins.

After collecting the suitcases, Fonseca Pereira took a taxi and told the driver to go up Avenida do Infante. The surrounding fields on either side of the road, with little houses to give some humanity to the landscape, were so different and gave him a strange feeling of being in another world. When they got to the Pináculo turn and Maria Pereira saw the city, an unexpected sight, she grabbed her husband's arm and confessed that it seemed more like a mirage than reality.

"I never imagined that Funchal would be so pretty!"

"You're right. The city has the sea and the mountains," observed Fonseca Pereira.

"What a pity we don't live here! And Armando and Carolina too."

The taxi quickly crossed Largo do Infante and stopped a few hundred metres down the road in front of an iron gate. They rang the bell. A servant appeared and asked what they wanted.

"Say that it's some friends," replied Maria Pereira.

After a moment, Inês, who was not aware of the surprise, saw her friends standing in the garden and could not believe that it really was them until she held them in her arms and felt the warmth of family feelings.

And after some strong emotion, she said, "What a pleasure you've given us! Are you staying for good?"

"We don't have that happiness!"

"Why not?"

"Life isn't only what we want it to be."

"Yes, that is true, my dearest friend."

But, with good will…!"

And while their conversation continued its spontaneous course, Francisco Freitas and Fonseca Pereira went into the downstairs sitting room.

"Inês, I've missed our evenings in Caracas!"

"And I've been dreaming almost every week about the walks we used to take!"

"I'm sad, Inês, when I remember things that can't be any more."

But turning from sad memories, she asked, "Where is Anabela?"

"She left early this morning with some friends to play golf at Santo da Serra. I'm very upset with her. The atmosphere in the city is very bad for her freedom loving character, and being her own mistress. She's completely different from Carolina."

"Listen, Inês, we must face life as it is. We're never as happy as we'd like to be."

"It still seems like a dream that you're here in my house, in your house, my dear friend. And how are our children, Carolina and Armando?"

"They were born for each other."

"And our grandson?"

"Your grandson looks like you, Inês. He has your eyes, just as intelligent."

"Mine! That's a friend exaggerating."

"No, it's not."

And Inês said to her husband, "Francisco, let's go and have lunch at the Savoy!"

"Maybe that's not a bad idea."

"It's just that here at home it would be very late."

Maria Pereira interrupted.

"Inês, do what you want. I'm not in charge here. I'm a guest."

"No, you're family!"

And they went upstairs.

"Here is your room. It was ours. The guest room is for guests…"

And while they were exchanging memories and going over the impressions that the Fonseca Pereira's had had during their first few hours in the city, they heard cars racing by and firecrackers exploding to announce the Madeira "Fair". Fonseca Pereira was amazed at the luxurious interior of the Savoy. He had visited many places around the world but he said to Freitas that the hotel where they were having lunch was better than any he had seen on his travels. The talk turned to the frivolous life of the city bourgeoisie, to whom money was the law and the values of the spirit were subordinated to that law. And because money rules men, the two industrialists went to the supermarket while Inês and Mrs. Maria stayed to talk endlessly about all that they had to say to each other after such a long time apart.

Fonseca Pereira was astounded by the length and the breadth of the shop, the profusion of articles of all kinds, both national and foreign, that filled the enormous space. There were four cash desks to deal with the customers who at that hour crowded into all the departments, which were stacked with merchandise.

"Come into the office, Mr. Fonseca."

And so, on the first floor, Alfredo got up from his desk chair to embrace the unexpected visitor to whom he had said a friendly farewell in Venezuela.

"Is your business doing well, Mr. Fonseca?"

"There have been changes since you were at the factory, my friend. I bought the land next door and put in new machines. Production has doubled. Sales are up. The needs of the country are increasing all the time."

"Here we're making a living. The island is small and there are a number of supermarkets in Funchal but I don't think there is one as big and as well stocked as ours."

One Sunday, when the sky was a clear blue and the mountain tops were tinged with bronze and so magical that it would be difficult to know whether the colours were real or figments of the imagination, the visitors acquiesced to Alfredo and Matilde's wish to go on a trip to the outskirts of the city, as far as Portela, if the weather was good. They left after a long visit to Inês's house, where the decorations, the furniture and the rare flowers in the small garden, the shapes, the colours and everything captivated them, and the bonds of friendship were strengthened still further in their subconscious.

The car sprang up the craggy side of the mountain that was dotted with terraces where the pine trees were bursting with sap. The view caught the attention of Maria Pereira and made her exclaim, "This is a gift from nature!"

But their fascination was complete when the visitors entered the woods on the Camacha farms.

"Here the action of nature is mixed with those of man," said Fonseca Pereira. "How is it possible for this land to have so many species of plant?"

"It was done by the English who were here in the last century. You have to acknowledge the fact that they were the agents of civilisation in these parts," observed Alfredo.

And after wandering around, with their eyes drinking in the sights, they were tempted to try the local wine. So, the car went straight to Santo and then, giving them only fleeting glimpses, along the zigzag road to Portela. The Penha d'Águia hill by the sea made Fonseca Pereira exclaim, "I don't have the words to say what I'm feeling!"

The sight of the little farms cultivated right up to where the cliffs drop down into ravines that bring terror to the eyes made Mr. Pereira opine, "If all the Island is like that, then the people have to emigrate. Now I understand why the Madeirans go to Venezuela, Canada, Australia and Brazil... Their hard work is barely enough to keep body and soul together."

That evening was spent at Matilde's and she did her utmost to entertain her friends at dinner. On the tables placed around the English-style drawing room and in the china cabinet, the plates shone in an exhibition that had all the airs of the *nouveaux riches*. On a plant stand was a strange box with a lid with a curious, inlaid picture of a mermaid. It had been given to Alfredo by the owner of a barber's shop in Antigua named João Anjo, who had been born and raised in the north of Madeira.

Anabela sat next to Maria Pereira with a disdainful expression on her face because she could not stand being with Raquel, Matilde's daughter. When she came to Funchal, Raquel and her mother visited each other in turn each week and spent the evening together. Anabela, however, thought the girl came from another, very chaste time, filled with outdated morality from days gone by and had an obsolete purity and provincial manners that set her teeth on edge. She told her mother how repellent she found Raquel. Inês tried in vain to convince her that she was wrong and hid the displeasure that she felt inside her. And on the day that Matilde invited her *comadre* Inês' family and the Fonseca Pereira's to dinner, when they were alone Anabela was put out and said that she would not leave the house. But Maria Pereira gave her some well thought out reasons why her attitude was inelegant and that her mother was very upset. So, she was there at the dinner, although it was hard for her and she felt constrained.

Matilde asked her if she would be soon be opening her consulting room and she replied that she still had not thought about her life seriously. The conversation became general and many topics were aired, from servants and the social life in Venezuela and on the Island to commerce and industry. And the champagne animated the conversation, which was mixed in with teasing and jokes.

Inês felt her irritation gnawing at her insides. That daughter had been born in Achada too but she did not have her blood or her soul. Not a week went by without her leaving the house in the morning to play golf or tennis, and she went to the Casino every night. Self-willed, decided in her actions, sacrificing herself for the dignity and the social position of the family, Inês felt remorse at not having conquered her failing of wanting to live and be someone in that remote time when business was falling off at the shop in Achada do Castanheiro.

Back at the Avenida do Infante, Anabela said good night to the Fonseca Pereira's and went to her room. Inês's mother's love was wounded and remembering Anabela's expression in Achada, she called out haughtily, "Anabela!"

The tone of her voice and the forcefulness of the request made Anabela open her door without delay.

"What is it, mother?"

"Are you going to bed without saying good night to me? Did your studies make you lose your love for your mother?"

"I'm sorry, mother." And she kissed Inês on her cheek.

***

The two families, with the addition of Matilde, went to the Reids Hotel, with its esplanade from where, on the night of St. Silvester, the singular spectacle of the lovely aurora borealis with its waves of multicoloured lights that twinkle in the sky captivates the gaze of visitors. The Fonseca Pereira's wanted the sensation of the changing lights to be repeated, as if virginity can be lived twice.

In the new year, Inês decided to take her friends to Achada where she had been born. Anabela thought that the day would be exhausting because the potholes that obstructed almost the entire length of the road made it hard for cars to get through.

In spite of everything, including Anabela's lack of good will, Inês's car, with Anabela at the wheel, took the two families to the north. Beyond the ring of the city, after the Poiso mountains, where there were no patches of fog on the high mountain peaks, and further on, in the mountain gorges that are here today and gone tomorrow, they saw the Cruzinhas and came to the whirlpools in the river valley. They went on and on and the Fonseca Pereira's were ecstatic, only speaking in monosyllables:

"Ah!" They could not get it out of their heads that the little road that runs along the irregular folds of the mountains was the original path cut by brave-hearted explorers.

On and on they went until they spied the sea that is there today as it always has been and went through a tiny hamlet that was there and gone in a flash. On another river bank with an unknown geographical history, the Volvo crossed a stone, cement and iron bridge. There below, the abyss told the eyes about the beginning of the world, a silent, Dantesque scene.

The car went by a building that exists only for the spirit, because its white bell tower was built only for the spirit.

Further and further on they went, by another river that sobbed out the human condition in its fatalistic waters that run away and never come back, just as what was lived yesterday can never be lived again today, until the car stopped in the little square of Achada do Castanheiro.

"Look, there's my father!" and the people of the village began to gather, looking timidly at the strangers.

"There's little Inês, who has a lot of possessions, thank God," commented a little old lady with a grey scarf on her head.

"Father, where's mother?" continued Inês. "That's my house, Mrs. Maria!"

"For you it's a holy relic, Inês. Keep it. It's worth as much as your great house in Funchal."

An old woman with a wrinkled face and wearing glasses was sitting at the door of a humble cottage, embroidering. Near her was a man, also quite old, sitting on a three-legged stool soling boots. He was wearing pyjamas. He had the look of a seafarer. Inês and her husband went up to him.

"Is that you, Mr. Artur?"

"Indeed, it is. I came back from Venezuela and here I'm staying. I could have had the luck that you had. I was one of the first emigrants from Achada. I ran around Brazil and set up shop in Venezuela, but I wasted all that I earned on women! My wife, Maria Clara, is still embroidering and I've gone back to my old trade."

At her grandparents' house, Anabela found a girl that she thought high spirited. So she talked to her. It was Isabelinha, who was in high school and was the parish school teacher. Achada impressed her more than the previous time, although she drew back from her grandmother's affection.

***

In January, the plants started to spring to life again.

As he visited the little plots of land, Fonseca Pereira understood that emigration was a necessity for the island. The people were enslaved to land that was so torn up that the furrows barely produced enough bread to feed them and provide them with clothing and shoes. And he chatted after lunch with Francisco Freitas, who described the financial outlook for the majority of the population of the north of the island: the crops are poor and so the people have to be poor.

Changing the subject, Fonseca Pereira reminded him that his friends would have their farewell lunch next day at the Savoy. Although she was interested in her conversation with her friend, Inês could not help hearing these words and immediately protested.

"While you're staying with us, you are our guests. And I won't let you leave yet."

"We've been here for two weeks and as happy as if we'd never been apart. But we have to leave. My husband can't be away any longer because we still have to go to Porto," said Maria Pereira. And she added, "I would have liked to spend more time with you, Inês. You know that's my greatest wish."

On the Thursday, a week before they left, Freitas and Inês invited their friends to dinner at the Romana, a typical restaurant in the old part of the city.

During dinner, they remembered with a tinge of emotion how fast the days had gone from sunrise to sunset in Venezuela. The coffee came and the conversation united them just as their weekly get-togethers in Caracas had.

"You know, Maria," said Inês, "Although I haven't mentioned the idea to you, I'm going to fulfil my life's dream and have a two-storey house built on that poor land where I was born."

Before Mrs. Maria could reply, Anabela cut in peremptorily:

"What nonsense! Wasting money in the countryside where anyone would die of boredom!" And with an expression of irritation on her face, she said, "I am completely against it. Why a house there, tell me, why there?"

Without growing angry, but disheartened, Inês replied:

"So that your grandparents can live in comfort for the rest of their lives and we can spend the summer and weekends there."

Francisco opened his eyes at his daughter as a sign of disagreement and did not say a word. Maria Pereira was stiff, almost petrified. Inês's eyes were wet. So, Anabela, to make her idea prevail, turned to Mrs. Pereira.

"Don't you think that I'm right? Burying money in that place…"

"Look, Anabela, I was born in a village on the Douro and I think about it when I'm tired of life. You have a very materialistic view of life, from a misspent youth. It's your parents who are right."

Anabela went red and lowered her eyes, biting her lip.

They went down the stairs in silence. The moon was lighting up a fold in the Corpo Santo square.

When they got home, Inês confessed to her friend that she was being destroyed by her great worry: Anabela had no feelings for her mother and she had turned out to be a degenerate daughter. It would have been better if she hadn't studied.

"I am so unhappy! In everyday life, I show what I'm not feeling. How much good it has done me to be with you every day, my dear friend! Sadly, I can see that nothing good ever lasts!"

The evening before they left, Maria Pereira shut herself up in her room with Anabela and spent more than an hour with her, without succeeding in proving that she had any sincere daughterly affection. Disappointed, she told Inês that she must have courage and resignation.

***

The Boeing 727 was due to take off in half an hour.

"I'll phone you from Porto, Inês, my friend." Their eyes were wet and their embrace was endless.

"And I expect to see you next year in Venezuela."

CHAPTER XXXII

EPILOGUE

Anabela was part of the social circle. She went to parties at the Casino, to tea at the English Club, was part of the cream of the bourgeois families and also never missed the medical conferences that were held from time to time in Madeira. She loved playing her favourite sport, tennis, at the Club and golf at the Santo da Serra course with foreigners and the young people who had studied at Coimbra and Lisboa.

However much Inês insisted that Anabela set up her consulting room in Rua da Carreira, she argued that she wanted to live her own life and she could live it very well without making use of her profession. Once, her father intervened in the matter at Alfredo's house but his daughter reacted with all the independence of her irreverent, rebellious and iconoclastic spirit. Matilde diplomatically tried to convince her, persuasively but in vain.

Inês recognised that living in the city was bad for someone of Anabela's temperament. She could not erect a dike to stem the habits that her daughter had acquired.

*****

Francisco Freitas received a letter from Jorge Ratazana that said,

"Caracas, January

"My good friend, Mr. Francisco,

"First of all, I must ask you to forgive me for only now replying to your letter, which was much appreciated. The reason for the delay was not only the hard work at the factory but also because I registered for a night class. As you know, the profits from the factory doubled starting in January. I must confess, my good friend and protector, that my savings are growing. A short time ago I moved to a much better house than where I used to live.

"My life is now such that I am very happy, except for the woman I married, who has never stopped being a village girl, I don't know why.

"I don't mean by this that she isn't good at everyday things. What I don't understand is holding on to life in the village, when she now has a nice house and good food and could get on, dress well and look like a lady. You know that she is unhappy and is always complaining about her back luck in living in Venezuela. Then I compare my life with Duarte's. His wife Lucinda spends time with her husband in his free moments and is even taking a course in business. Excuse my going on, but Rosa is disheartened. She wants to go home. And I feel sorry for her. I try to make her see that if things are good, one should let them be. And one day soon we'll go to Achada and then come back to Caracas. But she persists in wanting to stay there forever. She's a stay-at-home.

"I forgot to say, Mr. Francisco, that I've become a Venezuelan citizen but I'm not giving up on my homeland. Duarte and Lucinda have done the same thing. Our interests depend on the government and we depend on the state and it needs the immigrant vote.

"Sometimes I remember home and Teacher Jorge who gave me a taste for reading. If it wasn't for him, I wouldn't have the books on my bedside table that Engineer Armando and Dr. Carlos are kind enough to lend me.

"When are you coming back, Mr. Francisco?"

After Freitas read the letter to Inês, she was sad, thinking about Rosinha's manner and how she couldn't change. Her feelings for her homeland were stronger than her love for her husband. At the same time, she was filled with joy thinking that Ratazana, Duarte and Lucinda were emigrants who had triumphed over their homesickness, which can kill the desire to succeed in a foreign country.

***

Business prospered at the São Paulo supermarket in Funchal and also the bakery in Caracas. Freitas was already thinking of a trip to Venezuela with his wife and daughter and spending some time with the Fonseca Pereira's. Inês had made good friends among the families that belonged to big business and outstanding people in the liberal professions. The friendship of the wife of Judge Melo had given her a name. However, Matilde was special because she was also a close friend of Maria Pereira.

In the midst of these thoughts, the post brought a letter from Carolina, in which she wrote that she was missing her homeland. She said,

"Dearest mother,

"I am very happy with Armando and our son has started to take his first steps.

"I keep thinking about you, mother, father and Anabela, and also my grandparents. I'd love to hug you all and have you close by."

After reading the letter, Inês almost cried because of Carolina's great affection for them and her love for her grandparents, and compared the tenderness of the one daughter with Anabela, who was so uninterested and so lacking in family feeling. And sadness clouded her face and made her feel bitter.

The Saturday after the letter arrived, Inês heard, or thought she heard, the drawing room clock strike four in the morning. As she was in doubt as to whether she had made a mistake, she lit the candle on the bedside table and looked at her gold wrist watch, which was always close to hand. She saw that she had clearly heard the chimes. She did not think that Anabela had come home yet. Desperately worried, she put on her dressing gown, went onto the veranda and sat down on the side facing the Avenue to wait for her daughter. Then a car broke the deep silence that enveloped all the objects, trees, houses, gardens and streets. A moment later, a car stopped right by the house, next to the lamppost. At the same time, in the mute calm of the night, she heard bursts of drunken laughter and slurred voices.

Not wanting to be seen, Inês moved away, went into the house and looked out into the street through the slats of the shutters. She felt as if she had been struck by lightning. A bearded man had his arms around Anabela's neck and was kissing her.

This was their farewell. Anabela opened the iron gate and then the mahogany door and went upstairs. She saw the light in her parents' room but as she was mistress of her own affairs, why should she tell them that she was coming home at four in the morning? Inês spent the rest of the night awake, thinking about her bad luck. She had talked to her daughter like a mother. And she asked herself if she shouldn't have continued to live in Venezuela until death came.

At lunch, since her husband had gone on a trip to Pico do Areeiro with two businessmen from the mainland, Anabela did not say a word. Her mother broke the silence and slowly asked:

"Did you read your sister's letter?"

"Yes. She didn't say anything of interest."

"But she is happy."

"So am I! Each to his own."

"Listen, my girl, you're old enough to think about how your life should be. Your sister made a good marriage and you're here. With your position as a doctor, you don't lack suitors."

"But I don't want them for that. Carolina got married because she's not up to date. She's old-fashioned. Today's women are free. To have a husband it's not necessary to have a church or even a registry office."

"Who put those ideas into your head? I can't believe that you were born in Achada do Castanheiro like your sister."

"Even in Venezuela some colleagues of mine thought like I do. It doesn't matter if I was born in Achada. My day is not yours."

"Daughter, times can change but the virtues that Christ taught remain the same."

"Come, come! Don't take it badly, mother. That's how I think."

Inês was dumbstruck. Anabela got up from her chair, went to the desk and put an Elton John record on the turntable. She sat down in an armchair to listen in complete relaxation, with the knowledge that the truth was the truth that she had in her mind, that her generation repudiated all the old social preconceptions.

***

In her room that night, Inês, who was a woman of rigid principles, honest, serious, the bearer of a moral and Christian heritage that came down from the first serfs who dug the land in the north of the Island, spoke to her husband with mortification on her face.

"Our Anabela is so different from Carolina! And from Carlos! They were all born in Achada. But Anabela has turned out badly. Her studies and her fellow students have turned her head. Carolina and Carlos remain close to their ancestors, with respect for the family. Anabela is independent, free, doesn't think of ever marrying, is thought by sensible people to be shameless, despises her family in Achada and, who knows, maybe even us, her parents, who raised her and made her a doctor. Wouldn't we have been happier, Francisco, if, instead of emigrating and getting out of our hollow in the mountains, we had lived a simple life in the village, digging the fields and looking after a calf? We made so many sacrifices as we went through the world, and our family life was always correct, with no entanglements. I am so upset. We have so much money and so many comforts, Francisco! And, in the end, for what? Was it worth it?..."

Funchal – Estoril
1978

Books, edited by
Maria de Fátima Gouveia Soares (*the Author's daughter*):

«**Francisco Bento de Gouveia (1873-1956)**» – biography of the father of Horácio Bento de Gouveia – 2000

«**Tabita**» – (*Project for a novel dated 1924*) – 2013.

Investigation of written articles in local newspapers and conferences from 1918 to 1983:

«**Escritos da Juventude *(1918–1929)***» – 2001
«**Escritos 2 *(1930–1939)***» – 2007
«**Escritos 3 *(1940–1949)***» – 2008
«**Escritos 4 *(1950–1959)***» – 2011
«**Escritos 5 *(1960–1969)***» – 2014
«**Escritos 6 *(1970–1983)***» – *(due May)* 2016

«**Round Trip – The Emigrant's Journey**» – 2016

Printed in Great Britain
by Amazon

31062930R00126